SANTÉ'S SECRETS

SANTÉ'S SECRETS

A DEEP DIVE INTO DEBAUCHERY

JADE GREEN

Santé's Secrets
Copyright © 2025 Sticky Novels LLC

All rights reserved. No part of this book may be reproduced, distributed, or transmitted in any form or by any means, electronic or mechanical, including photocopying, recording, or by any information storage and retrieval system, without prior written permission from the publisher, except in the case of brief quotations used in critical reviews or articles.

Published by:
Sticky Novels LLC
201 York Road, Suite 1-522
Jenkintown, PA 19046

Copyright@StickyNovels.com

Visit our website at **StickyNovels.com**

Disclaimer:
This novel is a work of fiction. Any reference to real people, events, establishments, organizations, or locations is intended solely to provide a sense of authenticity. Names, characters, incidents, and events are either the product of the author's imagination or are used fictitiously.

This narrative is not meant to serve as an accurate historical account but rather as a fictional exploration inspired by certain real-world themes. The inclusion of specific themes or parallels to real-world events is for narrative purposes only and is not meant to reflect actual historical accuracies or the real-life actions of individuals. Readers should approach this work as a creative exploration, where the blend of fact and fiction serves to craft a compelling story, not a historical record.

Any resemblance to actual persons, living or dead, is purely coincidental. This work does not intend to infringe upon any individual's right of publicity or privacy. No real persons, living or deceased, have knowingly been depicted, nor does this work make any factual claims about any such individuals.

ISBN:
979-8-9903585-7-7 (Hardcover Uncensored)
979-8-9903585-2-2 (Paperback Uncensored)

Library of Congress Cataloging-in-Publication Data
Library of Congress Control Number: 2025903914

Santé's Secrets

BISAC Codes:
FIC056020 FICTION / Hispanic & Latino / Erotica
FIC005010 FICTION / Erotica / BDSM
FIC031080 FICTION / Thrillers / Psychological

Credits:
Story Created By: Jade Green
Book Cover Concept: Jade Green
Book Cover Design: CapriAGE

Printed in the United States of America

First Edition: April 2025

10 9 8 7 6 5 4 3 2 1

READER ADVISORY

THIS IS THE UNCENSORED EDITION OF THE NOVEL, SANTÉ'S SECRETS. This novel was created by and for adults and intended for audiences aged 18 years and older. This work of literary erotica contains explicit sexual depictions, mature themes, and separately references violent subject matter. It is not suitable or intended for readers under 18 years of age.

Themes of promiscuity, sexual narcissism, BDSM erotica, adult psychological drama, psychological thriller, and psychological suspense subject matter are depicted in explicit detail. This edition includes profanity, coarse language, and vulgar expressions.

For readers under 18 or adults seeking a more carefully calibrated edition of this literary work, the Censored Edition of Santé's Secret is available under the same title. You can obtain it in bookstores by special order (**ISBN**: 979-8-9903585-9-1) or purchase it directly at StickyNovels.com.

Everything positive I am, or will ever be, is because of my father. I will love you for the duration of my life and through the timeless existence of my spirit.

This novel is dedicated to my father,

Joe Young
1934–2025

May you rest in heavenly peace.

PROLOGUE

The past is a bitch you can't fuck anymore. My life has been a whirlwind of passion and mistakes. For me, Victoria Robbins was my lifelong passion and ultimate mistake. Years ago I rekindled my old flame with Victoria despite my marriage to Jackie.

Victoria fell hard for me, but it wasn't just love for her; I became her obsession. My dick turned that bitch out something crazy. Victoria wanted me so bad, she dug up dirt on my wife, then found a way to show me proof of her cheating, all without me knowing where the information came from.

Victoria's plan worked; angered and betrayed, I divorced my wife, Jackie Sabatino, and brought Victoria into my home, expecting her to step into my ex-wife's shoes and serve my every need.

But the pressure of my demands proved too much for her. Victoria ran from my house like a runaway slave, and in my foolishness, I chased her. We clashed in a fateful encounter where her green eyes, once full of love, suddenly had a wild, crazed look.

I never expected her to shoot me, but she did, and fucked up my shoulder. My ex-wife appeared soon after, calling the police. I took the stand in court as a witness against Victoria, sealing her fate to prison. She's out now, but she hasn't tried to reach me. Yet her mark remains with me, both physically and emotionally.

That was back in 2018, when life had a different rhythm, and I was moving to another beat. At twenty-nine, the days were mine to seize, full of sex and secrets. Now, at thirty-two, talk of Victoria doesn't roll off my tongue much, and my marriage finally ended for good two years ago.

Despite giving it one more try, I couldn't forgive Jackie for cheating on me, and I couldn't stop cheating on her. Worse, she kept catching me. I may not have had Jackie or Victoria in my life anymore, but I did have my memories. They stick around. It really freaks me out how my life with those two women continues to shape my present in quiet, unexpected ways.

You couldn't have convinced me back then that the shadows of my past would come back to dance in my present. Years of swagger and smut stories were usually saved for my homies, shared in the sacred confessional for men, the locker room. But the wildest parts of my freak life… those details stayed in the depths of my memory. Meant only for one man's enjoyment—mine… Santé Sabatino.

Never in a million turns of the earth did I think my rawest, most freaky escapades would get thrown into the daylight, for all to see. But then came 2021, a curveball year, when a random introduction swung open the gates to my most closely held secrets: Santé's Secrets.

*She fell into his eyes like deep water—
by the time she surfaced, she was already on her knees.*

CHAPTER ONE

SANTÉ'S KINGDOM

"There's nothing ever so wrong with me that a good blow job can't fix." That's what I wanted to type, staring at the endless questions on that damn medical form. Why had scheduling a simple doctor's appointment started to feel like solving a riddle?

I leaned back in my black leather chair, the cool, smooth surface pressing against my skin, and glanced around my kingdom. My dining room's dove-gray walls and polished sandalwood floors still gleamed as though I'd just bought the place yesterday, not three years ago.

The soft light in my kitchen hit just right, giving everything a clean, organized look that anyone would envy. Who says a divorced guy can't keep a tidy home?

Sure, the basketball in the corner gave off a bachelor vibe, but the rest? Spotless stainless steel appliances, a gleaming gray-and-white backsplash. Nobody would guess that, in over a year, no woman had stayed in my house longer than it took for me to empty my balls. Well, maybe forty-eight hours, if she let me fuck her up her ass for most of her stay.

The point is, my home wasn't just a place—it was a symbol. A shrine to my independence, a testament to the fact that I didn't need anyone to make my life work.

I'm not like most modern guys, the type of guy afraid to be a man. I make no apologies for having a dick and, according to my bitches, a pretty big one. My name is Santé Sabatino, Latino lover, dominator, and master to many.

But on the Saturday afternoon of May 1, 2021, I was just a dude trying to set a fucking doctor's appointment using my laptop because the phone app was for shit.

The dull ache in my shoulder made every click of the keyboard echo in my head like a basketball smackin' the court, even though the ball just lay there silent in the corner.

After the fifth error message, I gave up. Fuck technology; I'd call later. Leaning back, I massaged my shoulder, the pain spreading like wildfire. Maybe it was from the pickup game last night. Or had I overdone it in the pool?

Then, a darker memory hit me. A flash of green eyes, a gunshot—Victoria. My hand drifted to the scar she'd left, a mark etched into my skin and my soul.

I shook off the memory and wandered toward the sliding glass doors leading to my backyard. Watching the sprinklers hiss and spray across the lawn, the scene moved in slow motion. Fluid. Forgiving. Maybe it's because I'm a Pisces, but water has always called to me. Something primal—a real turn-on.

Water wasn't just water to me. It was a force that erased mistakes, washed away flaws, and left nothing but purity in its wake. Every time water touched my skin, it felt like I was getting a fresh start, cleansing me from the deeds of my darker moments. A baptism for sins I'd refused to name, and for lust I couldn't tame.

The rhythm of water hitting the earth reminded me that no matter how dirty things got, there was always a way to get clean. To be restored. Lost in the display of dancing droplets, time seemed to stretch and bend.

The hiss of the sprinklers slowed time, but then, reality snapped back. The mail. *Shit!* Collecting mail was one of those things my ex-wife Jackie used to do. Now, I ran my house myself, which meant stuff like going to the mailbox was my job.

Grumbling, I made my way to the laundry room. I enjoyed the sound of my dick slapping against my thighs as I moved—ultimate freedom. My house was my domain. No rules. No interruptions. Just me.

For a brief second, I toyed with the idea of strolling to the curb free-balling; then, I had second thoughts.

I thought my suburban neighbors might not appreciate the Big Dick Papi experience. This was Turnersville, New Jersey, after all, not Philly, my urban birthplace, where a bold display might be appreciated—or, if not, at least respected.

So, I grabbed a pair of blue ball shorts instead. I chuckled. My dick print was still visible, even though I wasn't even semi-hard; what can I say? I'm Santé Sabatino—dick-blessed.

I thought; *If anyone had a problem with me—or that reality... fuck 'em, literally—fuck 'em.*

Taking a deep breath, I swung open the front door and stepped outside, the sun hitting my skin like a welcome dare. Whatever waited out there, I was ready to conquer.

Two steps outside of 32 Pond Drive, the dove-gray siding of my house caught the last light of the peach-toned sun. No matter how many times I looked at it, pride swelled in my chest. This was mine—earned, owned, and thriving.

My worn tan Suburban sat in the driveway like a battle-scarred champion. That truck had seen more pussy in the back seats than the average gynecologist's office. It was also the ride that hauled groceries for my kids when we had nothing else, and it was still kicking.

Not bad for a Puerto Rican kid from North Philly who folks thought was dumb and wouldn't make it past twenty-five outside of a prison cell. Now, I was living the dream—my dream. The house, the truck, the single life. Divorce was the best thing that ever happened to me.

Let's face it, I was a catch. Thirty-two, handsome as hell, good job, nice house, and a good-paying job.

I had it better than most men on my block. I had my kids every other weekend and a bigger pussy parade than guys in their twenties could dream of.

I didn't even bother to smash most of the smuts I hooked up with at my house. I'd usually just pull out my dick on some side street, or in an alley, slide on a condom, and fuck the freak of the moment until she was more foolish than she was before she hopped in my truck. Then I'd leave her in a ball of dust, with my truck's exhaust fumes up her nose and the bitter-sweet aftertaste of my cum dancing on her tongue.

No invitations to my crib were left; instead, most of the random sluts were left with throbbing pussies and one of my many disposable cell phone numbers. Little did they know I changed those app-based phone digits more often than they changed the winning Powerball lottery numbers. Nawh, my house—was mainly for me and my peace of mind.

I walked down the concrete path toward my driveway, the sun warming my skin and fueling my confidence. I was the man. No doubt about it.

That's when the sprinklers kicked on with a sharp click and hiss, spraying me in the chest with cold, stinging jets. I flinched at the icy water beads rolling down my skin, half-annoyed, half-awake from the jolt.

I made a mental note: *fix the damn sprinkler system. Cheap hoses weren't cutting it anymore.*

Then, a sharp yelp turned my head. Across my property line, a woman danced around the sudden spray of water. She had light auburn curls that caught the sunlight, denim shorts that skimmed over long, lean legs and a blue v-neck shirt just barely holding back those full round titties. The cleavage was barely closed, hanging on by the mercy of one overworked button.

I caught myself staring at that button, half-wondering if it would survive the raucous titty bouncing.

Shaking it off, I sprinted to shut off the spigot by my house. From the corner of my eye, I caught her dodging the sprays with surprising grace and rhythm. Her laughter mixed with the hiss of the sprinklers. The water slowed to a stop, the hose deflated, and I walked back toward her, the lawn still glistening from its unintended shower.

She stood on the edge of the lawn and her walkway's border, her golden skin catching the light just right. I tilted my head slightly, letting the sun hit my eyes. Women always noticed my eyes—amber and sea-foam green with flecks of red. When sunlight hit my eyes, pussies tended to get wet. I knew it, and I used it.

"Damn, really sorry about that," I said, letting my chest glisten in the fading sunlight. "Overzealous sprinklers, you know?"

She smirked. "Well, that's one way to get a girl's attention."

My eyebrows arched in mock surprise. "Oh? It worked?"

She laughed and replied, "Sorta." During a pause, I noticed her white teeth as she smiled. The attractive stranger asked, "So, you're in 32?"

It took me a few seconds to realize she was talking about my address.

Once I caught on, I said, "That's right. And you're occupying 30 now?"

She nodded and replied, "Yeah, I just made settlement on the place recently. Still have a lot of unpacking to do."

We had drifted to the middle of the lawn, stopping just at the edge of our property lines. That's when I got a better look at the beauty before me. Kissed by the sunlight, her skin was warm and golden—smooth as silk. The curves of her face highlighted her high cheekbones, giving her an elegant look but still somewhat down-to-earth.

Her eyes weren't as sexy as mine, but, man—with those big, almond-shaped, cherry-brown beauties, I was sure she'd been breaking hearts for a while.

She had perfectly arched eyebrows, and her nose was delicate. Her moving lips were full and naturally rosy. The upper lip curved gently, while the lower lip was round and inviting. I thought: *The perfect place to tap the head of my dick.*

I grinned as she spoke about some shit I didn't really care about. But I did appreciate her down-to-earth beauty. She had the package: her eyes, her smile, and everything about her was just magnetic.

After a moment, I realized she seemed to be waiting for a response. Since I had no damn clue what she had been rattling on about, I couldn't reply even if I had wanted, so I hijacked the conversation.

"Well, if you ever think of welcoming your neighbor with a cake," I said with a playful wink, "I'm big on vanilla icing and Medalla Light beer."

The sexy stranger's eyebrows quirked in amusement, and she said; "Not exactly an answer to my question, but intriguing." She put her hand on her hip and asked, "Wait, isn't the older neighbor usually supposed to welcome the newbie?"

"Well, I never play by the rules," I answered with a smirk.

I could tell she was taking a moment to consider both my words and my swagger before announcing, "My name's Amanda, by the way."

I suggested, "Amanda... Is too formal for cake-sharing neighbors. How about Manda?"

Amanda tilted her head, her cherry-walnut peepers sparked with amusement. "Manda, huh? I suppose I can live with that," she said before asking, "And what should I call you?"

"Santé... you can call me—Santé," I replied.

"Okay, Santé, nice to meet you," Amanda said before turning to leave.

From her flushed, rosy cheeks, I could tell what I said next caught her off guard. "By the way, next time? It's your turn to get us wet."

As Amanda laughed slyly, I caught the faintest hint of resemblance to one of my favorite singers, Mariah Carey. Her laughter had a warm, rich tone. She sashayed toward her new home, her voice fading as she said, "I hope you'll be ready for the splash zone."

Chuckling, I kept watching Amanda walk away. *I'm always ready for the wet action,* my inner voice replied. 'Manda' had a phat ass, just as I liked. From years of donating dick to both the needy and the greedy, my experience gave me confidence that Manda's ass cheeks would spread easily as soon as she bent over, providing a perfect view if I fucked her from behind.

Suddenly, I remembered why I had come outside—the mail. I marched down the driveway to the curb and reached into the mailbox. My mind was half on the mail and half on Manda. I grabbed the envelopes and kept sneaking glances next door. Amanda was slipping into her house with a smooth, feminine motion that made my dick twitch.

Heading back to my front door, I considered how my new neighbor might add some fun to my life. Those thoughts stayed

JADE GREEN

with me as I stepped back inside my kingdom, the sunlight drying the last water droplets playing on my bare skin.

*She fell into his eyes like deep water—
by the time she surfaced, she was already on her knees.*

CHAPTER TWO

THRILLS OVER BILLS

Bills, bills, and more fucking bills. I was damn mad. I was pissed that I had even made the short trip to the mailbox. Every single envelope was a fucking bill. I slung the handful of envelopes across my dining room table.

The only thing more expensive than my marriage was my divorce. I had all my house bills and child support. I was still making payments to my lawyer, who helped me get joint custody, pay no alimony, and make sure Jackie couldn't force me to sell my home.

But my ex-wife was still a ticking time bomb, ready to grab half the money if I ever sold my crib. Since I had no plans to leave Pond Drive anytime soon, I knew I could deal with that headache later.

My main focus was on stacking cash. I still looked like I was in my twenties, so I thought modeling gigs would be my best shot at quick money. The problem with that plan was that my best shot at modeling gigs was through my ex, Victoria Robbins. Victoria was a former modeling agent and fancy TV executive.

But our connection of more than a decade didn't work out. I gave her dick to suck on—she fell in love. I took her virginity—she gave me her soul. I pulled away to save my marriage; she snapped.

Long story short, she wanted me so bad she wormed her way into my bed by deception. When I learned about her deceit, I firmly put her back in her place as just my sex toy, but... I may have gone too far. That's when the bitch shot me. The bottom line is that she's probably a no-go on the modeling reference.

So, I had to focus on getting more out of my bread and butter—my welding gig. I was damn good at it, skilled as hell, and knew my worth. That is why I knew it was time for a raise, or even better, a promotion and a fatter paycheck.

The shop supervisor spot had been on my mind for the past week. I'd been scheming how to snatch that title for myself, but I hadn't worked out a full plan. I heard my father's voice in my head. *This is your life; take the risk and enjoy the rewards. You don't get points for politeness in the grave; make your time matter.* Just like that, the pain of my dad's death crept in.

I felt my eyes sting, so I manned up and shut down the temporary emotional moment. Dad was in a better place, with no bills to worry about. I sank onto my black leather couch, soaking in the sweet chill from the central air.

I kicked off my blue and white Nikes, feeling the cool touch of the wooden floor under my feet. Man, that felt good. I looked down at my size twelves and smiled. I thought of Karina and her obsession with my feet. *That was one freak bitch*, I thought.

Visions of Karina rubbing my bare feet all over her face while she played with her pussy came to mind. The six months I fucked her while her dude was in jail returned to my mind like it was yesterday. I sat up straight, realizing it had been two years since that bitch begged to suck on Daddy's toes. At that moment, I made another mental note: *Add a new foot freak to my roster of hoes.* I considered whether Holly could fill the position.

I crashed back onto the couch, mentally arranging and prioritizing my bitches in their proper order, according to freak skills and submissiveness; work was the last thing on my mind. Then my boss called, ringing my phone like an unwelcome alarm clock in my brain. It felt like getting hit with a cold bucket of reality in the middle of a dream.

What the hell does this motherfucker want, especially on my day off.

Answering my cell, I said, "Joel, man, wasn't expectin' to hear from you today. What's up?"

Joel's familiar voice hit my ear, "Santé, my man. Heard you got your eyes on that supervisor gig?"

The shop supervisor gig had been on my mind all week. I knew my worth, and no way I was settling for less.

"You know it. Time I took the lead, right?" I said.

A small laugh poured from the phone. "Sure thing," Joel said. "But it ain't just about being the cool guy, y'know?"

"I hear you," I said, feeling my annoyance rise. I hated when motherfuckers talked down to me. Why do they all think I'm dumb? I figured it was some racist stereotype shit, 'cause I'm Puerto Rican.

There was straight-up silence for a minute, but I was cool with the tension. I hoped he'd think twice about his words. Then, Joel said, "Let's chop it up Tuesday morning, alright? Talk about this whole promotion thing."

"You outta the office on Monday?" I asked.

"Yeah, got this church thing in Pittsburgh."

I chuckled. "Praying on a Monday? That's so you."

Joel admitted, "Yeah, you got me on that one. God, family, business, and reputation. That's what matters to me." he quickly added, "Of course, there's Jenga."

For a second, I wondered; did *Joel just slip up and name his side bitch?* Then I remembered he was talking about some crazy-ass kids' game of stacking wood pieces.

I asked, "So you're still stacking those wood blocks, huh?"

Joel laughed, "You know it! It's like meditation for me. I got ten completed Jenga towers at home and I'm working on two at work."

Man, this mother-fucka's a psycho, I thought before letting my professional voice speak.

"Man, you and your crazy games," I shook my head and asked. "Ever thought of entering some kind of competition or something with that?"

"One day," Joel promised, chuckling.

After we hung up, I couldn't help but think Joel was just a straight-up asshole. But I did like the sound of becoming the shop supervisor of Manning & Mercer Containers. I was going to get that promotion one way or another, and the mission would start on Tuesday.

Then, a more pressing matter hit me. I reached for my phone and shot off a quick text to Kay, typing three lines back to back so she'd get three notifications:

> Joel's out tomorrow.
> His office will be ours for fuckin.
> Lunch? I'm serving DICK!

I put my phone back in my ball shorts. I thought: *that handled Monday's fuck-and-suck-session,* but my dick was hungry again, at least around the tip. I checked the clock; shit—I was late.

I grabbed my basketball from the room floor. Better not be too late for the game. And Holly? She better be there. After ten hours of no action, I needed one of her wet blowjobs—for real.

*She fell into his eyes like deep water—
by the time she surfaced, she was already on her knees.*

CHAPTER THREE

THREADS OF AN ALLIANCE

"I don't know if he's a psycho, but damn, he's sexy." Those were the first words I blurted out to Isaac Scott over Skype right after meeting Santé, and Isaac freaked out.

Isaac's face morphed from curiosity to concern in a heartbeat. The lean lines of his athletic frame shifted slightly as he sat up straighter in his chair. His deep brown eyes, usually full of warmth, now reflected caution as they locked onto mine through the screen. His neatly trimmed goatee, always impeccable, framed his mouth, and his smooth, cocoa-brown skin, flawless as ever, seemed to darken with worry. "Amanda, seriously? This is supposed to be professional. No, girl, let's call this off. I have a bad feeling about this. Santé Sabatino is trouble best avoided."

His voice streamed through the speakers, smooth and sure, while I sat in my small office nook. I glanced at the full-length mirror to my left, catching a glimpse of my reflection—my light auburn curls cascading over my shoulders, framing the subtle glow of my sun-kissed golden skin. It wasn't just the warmth of the spring air that made my face shimmer today. The excitement of meeting Santé had left me with a radiance I hadn't seen in years.

Isaac's voice, still brimming with concern, snapped me back. "Are you even listening to me?" His brow furrowed within the pixelated image on my screen.

I met his gaze, a reluctant smile playing on my lips. "I hear you, Isaac. I'm just saying the man is FYNE!" I emphasized the word, letting my naturally rosy lips curve into a playful grin. "But that doesn't mean I'll let my guard down."

His face relaxed a little, though he still seemed on edge. Isaac always had this way of showing his emotions through his expressions—whether it was his wide smile that lit up his mahogany skin, or the way he now furrowed his brow in disapproval. "I'll tell you one thing," I added, leaning closer to the camera, "They're right when they say black don't crack. You look flawless."

Isaac offered a small smile, but his eyes remained serious. "Don't try to distract me with flattery, Mandy. I know you know your craft."

I straightened in my chair, brushing a hand through my curls, which seemed to bounce back with a life of their own. "My craft is getting to the truth, Isaac, and that is perfectly consistent with the Santé mission."

Isaac's smile dropped, but the sharp angles of his high cheekbones remained prominent as he leaned back dramatically. "Girl, Santé is a bad boy, and your bad boy Santé reminds me of my former bad boy."

A chuckle escaped me. "If you make me talk about that man again, I'll have to charge you my standard rate."

Isaac gasped dramatically, eyes widening in mock horror. "Bitch, no, you didn't. My good, good Judy doesn't charge me for her services."

We always fell into this rhythm—Isaac's animated, fluid gestures filling the screen, my teasing remarks easing the tension between us. But in truth, we held each other accountable for our actions. It had been that way since our first year of college.

"Calm down, Your Majesty. I'm not going to actually charge you." I grinned. "But I also don't want to relive your obsession with the man you yourself have said was married… to a woman."

Isaac's playful demeanor dropped momentarily, his face frozen on the screen. But to his credit, he responded with uncharacteristic restraint. "I am smart enough to know this situation is not about my former 'trade'. I also know the importance of our plan. But with that said, both 'J' and Santé appear to be the same type of man, and you can never let your guard down or allow your feelings to get involved."

I watched Isaac closely as he spoke, noting how his face softened, the sharp lines of his jaw relaxing just a bit. He always had this way of making his emotions so visible, whether in person or over a screen.

"Mandy, as always, I've got your back, just protect us from the front. Santé Sabatino is not someone to be trifled with."

I took a deep breath, leaning back in my chair. "I know what I'm doing, Isaac. Trust me."

As the call ended, his image faded from the screen, leaving me alone with the power of his words. The reflection in the mirror caught my eye again—my almond-shaped eyes still bright, though clouded with doubt. Whatever lay ahead, I was in it now, fully and irrevocably.

CHAPTER FOUR

GAME OVER, BITCHES

All eyes were on me, as they should be. After all, whose face was plastered on every flyer and promotional piece for the league? Santé Sabatino, of course. The one shot of me—palming a basketball, my signature eyes locked on the camera with unshakable intensity—had become iconic.

That image wasn't just on game pamphlets; it was everywhere—on banners, on the team's website, even on the backs of ticket stubs. The league was eating it up, just like the crowd was eating me up.

And on that Saturday night—the first of May—they couldn't get enough.

I loved everything about that night. From the way my tight, number six jersey hugged my skin, clinging to the sweat and adrenaline, to the one-on-one action after the game.

No doubt, it was my night.

I was flexing my muscles, and everyone loved the view—especially the horny bitches in the stands.

I was a one-man storm on that basketball court—untouchable.

Me and my boys, the Turnersville Titans, were a yellow-and-black blur, moving lightning fast, putting a SmackDown on those bitch-ass Camden Comets.

From the word go, I could tell the Camden Comets couldn't tell their asses from holes in the ground. They were a disaster, a blur of red and black, scrambling like headless chickens. Their plays were all confusion and chaos. Their frantic scurries and desperate lunges did zilch to pull them from the hole they were digging themselves into.

The squeaks from the Titans' sneakers and the heavy thuds of the basketball hitting the plywood filled the electric air. I controlled the ball like a master. The b-ball's steady bounce showed the power running through my veins; everyone could see I was king.

My arms moved the ball with a swagger. Every dribble and pass was a silent challenge to the competition. Even in the fourth quarter, my focus was laser-sharp, only breaking to steal a glance at Holly Deever, my eager beaver in the stands. Each time I looked for her, she was staring back at me hungrily. Holly's boyfriend and my former teammate Jake looked in my direction, but less at me and more at the entire game.

It was a shame he couldn't see the actual game was right in front of his face, and the player was the slick bitch holding his hand. Holly and I both knew that as soon as I finished dominating the basketball game, I would be dominating her tonsils with a strong face-fuckin'.

If we had time, I also planned to dip my dick into that brown-skinned pussy; for both pleasure and principle. The principle was always the same. The most important principle of all — because I was Santé motherfucking Sabatino...so I could.

As I lined up for the next play, I glanced in Holly's direction again. She was looking. She licked her lips as she held Jake's hand. The corner of my mouth tipped upward, but I forced myself not to smile, even though I knew that same hand Jake held would soon be cupping my balls. The lips she was licking would shortly be wrapped around my eleven-inch dick.

The players returned to motion, and I knew I had to wrap things up on the court. The game was nowhere near close; the Turnersville Titans were spanking the Camden Comets' asses, and all of them knew it.

I dribbled past one of the Camden Comets' better players, Tyson, a tall, lanky, dark-skinned brotha who always had a chip on his shoulder. "Call me professor 'cause I'm about to teach," I shouted, weaving between two more players. The three-point line was right there, and I knew what I had to do. Planting my feet, I launched the ball, my eyes locked on it as it arced perfectly and swished through the net.

"That's how it's done!" I roared, my heart bangin' hard against my ribcage. I smashed my fist against my chest, feeling like the king I was. The court was abuzz; cheers and jeers erupted from the stands. The place was filled with a blend of youth, culture, and sheer excitement. I soaked it in—all that noise and praise—all for me.

In the first quarter, my sweat slid down my brow, but by the fourth quarter, I could taste beads of sweat in my mouth; the salty juice only increased my concentration with each pass, dribble, and pump fake.

Within seconds, the ball was mine again, snatched from the Camden Comets' number twenty-one with a quick, rough grab.

My heart was pounding, but all I could hear was the crowd going wild as I tore down the court. Red and black jerseys tried to stop me, but my feet were too fast, and my eyes were locked on that basket. Tension built with every bounce, every step closer. Everyone was watching, waiting. The crowd rose as I jumped, launching the ball with pure will and muscle. Swish!

Three seconds later, the game buzzer rang; *game over, bitches*! The Turnersville Titans won 102 to 68. My teammates surrounded me, their hands delivering pats of brotherly love on my back, exuberant in our victory.

The sad puppy dog faces of the Camden Comets only added to my sense of triumph and gave me a semi-erection, a head start for my post-game private party with Holly.

"Yo, Mike!" I called to one of my teammates. "Do me a favor, keep Jake busy for a sec, will ya?"

With a curious tilt of his head, Mike asked, "Why?" Then he glanced into the stands, spotting Holly Deever stepping away from Jake, leaving him standing alone.

Mike's sarcasm flared, "Wat'cha bout to fuck his girl or something?"

I looked at the time, 9:35 P.M., then looked at Jake before replying, "Since I only have about ten minutes, probably more-like... something." I smirked.

I could see the recognition of my devilish intention on Mike's face. I saw his shocked reaction and his open-mouth expression. As the revelation of my ballsy courage penetrated his mind. His stunned look of amazement and awe added to my pleasure, and the stiffness of my hard-on. I knew it was only a matter of time before I would be sporting some heavy wood. I had to leave the basketball court immediately.

Making my move off the court, I yelled, "Do me this favor." Seemingly at a loss for words, Mike simply nodded in agreement.

My gaze tracked Holly weaving through the crowd, heading toward the bathrooms. I knew that it was her practiced fake-out. The bathrooms were just out of the basketball court doors. Once out of sight, I knew she was planning to leave the building.

I made my way to the side door leading directly outside to the baseball area. Making my move towards the shadows of the dugout, my dick was rock hard—ready for action.

CHAPTER FIVE

LIQUID LUST

The water first ran down my chest, calming my restless energy; by the time the warm trickles reached my balls, I was practically tranquil. The smell of the chlorine from the nearby pool tickled my nostrils. It was time for a swim.

The wall clock hit 10:15 P.M., over an hour after the Clearwaters Swim Club should've been dark and silent. But there I was, swaggering from the showers to the main pool's edge, my long dick swinging, my wide smirk gleaming in the peaceful quiet. It had been over five years since I began fucking Carol, the club's manager, but it was still one of my best moves. How else could I swim after hours, alone and unbothered? Only half of the lights were on, adding to the chill mood.

The surface of the large pool looked like a wet, glassy mirror. Looking at my handsome image, I wiggled my toes against the tile underneath me. I sucked in a breath and jumped into the water with force. Bubbles scrambled around me, shooting up while I zipped under the surface. Popping back up, I got to work, arms slicing through the water, legs kicking like they had a mind of their own.

Every time, it was the same drill. The muscle, the power, each lap, reaching each end of the pool. But it never took too long before that familiar mental slip started. My body would slowly feel distant, like it was moving and swimming, all on its own, without needing the "me" part anymore. My mind's eye would kick in, lighting up with images of scenes from my sexual escapades.

Usually, it would be flashes of my last sexual encounter that play in sharp focus. Crisp and vivid dick sucks, the smell of fresh pussy, even the sensation of ass banging. Kinda like watching an instant replay of a game.

Even though it's happened hundreds of times, I was always amazed; the shift from the vigorous physical swim to a dreamlike state of a fuck and suck show; so genuine, so enticing, and sooooooo—addictive.

As if on cue, images of Holly Deever from a few hours earlier flashed within the splashing water. Holly's plump titties bounced as she ran toward me, covered only by her yellow shirt.

I said, "You're such a whore, you don't even have a bra on. I can see your hard nipples poking out". As I suspected, my raunchy talk didn't insult Holly; she smiled and fell to her knees. With no complaints, Holly yanked my ball shorts down; my dick jumped out and smacked her on the lips. I loved when that happened, not just with Holly; it happened with lots of my sluts, and their reactions were usually a mix of surprise and submission.

I wasted no time; I positioned Holly's head against the dugout wall. I reached down and lifted her shirt. Her plump brown tits and light pink areolas leaped out to greet me properly. I could tell her nipples were sensitive because she jumped and closed her mouth around my big bicho each time I rubbed them.

The water rushing over my bare dick during my laps back and forth reminded me of Holly's wet mouth. The rush I felt as her tongue moved around the head of my dick was everything I wanted at that moment.

I jammed my tool into the back of her throat; neither of us had time to play. It didn't take long for her to choke, but I knew from our past experiences and her previous text messages—she loved it.

I remember closing my eyes; there was an image of water, the same water that was right there in front of me in the pool. Bubbles, waves, and all that motion, just dancing around in the darkness behind my eyelids.

The choking and slurping kept my dick rock hard. Holly cupped my balls like I had trained her to do over our many sessions, which started almost a year before. I wanted to fuck her, but I knew that would push our time limits.

With my black ball shorts down around my ankles and her head against the wall, I went to town, pumping her mouth and throat. Holly's saliva was everywhere. Before long, my dick was drenched with Holly's throat slime. Long strands streamed from my saturated balls and dripped onto her yellow shirt—a souvenir for her and Jake.

The sound of my moans merged with the sound of the bubbles in the pool. I could see myself pulling my wet dick from Holly's mouth and playfully slapping her with it. Holly giggled with delight. I pushed my man meat back into her mouth. My toes curled slightly. My body warmed, and beads of sweat formed on my forehead.

We were about eight minutes in, and with only two minutes to spare, I knew I was about to cum.

I could almost feel the small trimmers just under my balls, just as I felt a few hours before, the memory of my climax clear; I could hear myself as I gasped for air in the dimly lit baseball dugout. Holly was practically hyperventilating when I finally removed my dick from the back of her throat.

In the pool's embrace, I could still hear Holly coughing from the sensation of choking. The vision was clear, heaps of my thick white cum coating her tongue. As I had taught her, she held my sweet nut juice on her tongue for my visual inspection and enjoyment. Seeing my seed shimmer from the pale moonlight above, I smiled, giving her a fraction of the validation she desperately wanted. She drank my cum almost as vigorously as she inhaled my approval. Within a second, she swallowed all of my protein treat.

Holly muttered something, but whatever she said, I quickly dismissed it when I heard Jake's voice in the distance. "Holly you out here?" She turned her head to look in the direction of the sound. I don't know if she ever turned back because I left the scene like a ghost in the night. Leaving her with a wet pussy, a wet mouth, but well-fed.

With the memory complete, I stopped swimming and placed my hand on the tile just above the pool's edge. I took a few deep breaths. Water dripped from my black curly hair, making light dribbling sounds as the droplets hit the pool. My body and mind had experienced a fantastic workout.

After a moment, I eased myself under the water, moving like a human submarine. This time, there was no splashing; the water above stayed smooth, chill, and peaceful. Pushing through the water from deep under the pool's center, I felt lighter, making me float slowly to the top. The soft trickling of water off my head felt like it was washing stuff away. I wasn't just relaxed; I was more than chill; I was reborn.

CHAPTER SIX

CONFUSING CRAVINGS:

Dear Diary,

I'm gonna have to make a decision soon. Jake or Santé? I think I'm in love twice. Jake is everything a girl could want from a boyfriend; he's usually kind. He buys me stuff and sends me text messages. My mother even likes him, and she hates everyone. But there's almost no sexual attraction.

Is that why I'm in love with Santé? With him, I'm caught in a cycle of lust and guilt. I told myself it was just a fling, a thrill, nothing more than sex. But each time I look into those eyes of his I feel something; warmth spreads from the inside out, something deeper than I ever meant to feel.

And the shocking part? I feel it just the same—whether he's standing in front of me or I'm just looking at his picture.

I swear, every time I see that famous close-up of Santé gripping a basketball, his handsome face staring into the camera—those eyes, like pools of a rainbow, shifting from amber to green with touches of red—Lord, I get weak.

Jake thought I kept the flyer because he used to be on the team. I couldn't tell him how often I stared at it for my own desires.

So how could I walk away from the real thing? The man behind those eyes—the man who looks at me the same way in the dark, in those stolen moments, or in the quiet glow of morning light, briefly connecting before he goes to work.

Looking down at me, his hands pulling me closer than I ever thought I'd be.

I want to be his. I want to be with Santé.

But then—after, he leaves. And my heart breaks a little more each time.

It's been almost a year now, and Santé has taught me a lot, mostly freaky shit. The fucked up part is I'm twenty-three years old, and a college graduate, but I still haven't learned how to really know if a man really loves me or ever will.

In every freaky text message from Santé, I hear a whisper that tells me maybe there's more to this, more to us. Plus, there's all the stuff he's taught me to do. I've learned how to suck his balls like he likes, and how to deep throat, though I still choke because I can't get his dick all the way down yet. I've learned how to breathe just right so I can make my pussy take more dick inside. I've even agreed to do something I'd never thought I'd learn to do—eat a man's ass.

I feel like you can't do all that stuff with somebody and not love them... at least a little bit, right?

But then I have to face how Santé treats me after he gets what he wants—ghosted, like I don't exist. Like last Saturday night, I almost got caught sucking Santé's dick in the baseball dugout.

Jake's still a little suspicious. I told him I got sick. How else would I explain all the spit on my shirt while being alone in the dugout?

I still don't know how Santé disappeared so fast. I guess it was a good thing, but I gotta admit, at that moment, I felt foolish, alone on my knees.

With Jake, he is more stable, so why do I crave the feelings I have when I do the secret sexual stuff with Santé?

Confused,
Holly

CHAPTER SEVEN

VANILLA ICING ON THE GAME

I had just pulled my dick out when my doorbell rang. I had intended to bust a quick nut to the porn I had been watching for the previous five minutes, but it seemed somebody wanted to fuck up my Sunday evening plans.

I didn't immediately turn off the fuck flick. Two bitches were sucking on a massive dick, but when the bell rang a second time, I looked at my red digital clock mentally documenting the exact moment my evening went to shit—7 P.M.,.

With hesitation, I pulled on a pair of my Tommy Hilfiger boxers and wrapped myself in the black and gold Versace robe Victoria had given me for my twenty-fifth birthday. Jackie, my wife at the time, never bought the lie that the robe was a gift from my mother—but I still kept the rope.

Dragging myself down the steps and to the front door, I was a bit ticked about missing the dick-sucking bitches on the screen, but then I got a surprise.

Through the door's center glass, I saw Amanda, my new, flirtatious neighbor from next door. She appeared to be holding a small vanilla cake with fluffy vanilla icing on a plate. She also had a teasing smile playing on her lips.

When I swung the door open, the sweet smell hit me right away, pulling my eyes down to the cake before snapping back to Amanda's face. My smile broke out easy and genuine. She remembered my likes. Good. I appreciate a woman who listens and isn't afraid to make the first move; it's proof she knows my worth.

Amanda's sharp attention to the vanilla icing and popping up out of nowhere sparked my interest. This could be fun.

"A pleasant surprise, this is," I said, keeping my eyes on her in a manner I knew would get most women wet. Her eyes twinkled with fun as she responded, "A bit of reverse hospitality."

Amanda handed me the cake and, laughing a little, continued, "It's yours. But if you want a cold Medalla Light, you'll have to come to my place for that."

Aww, this bitch's got game, I thought. Not too much, just the right amount. Something about her easy charm and dick-sucking lips made me want to play along. I glanced at the cake, then back at Amanda; lightly touching the corners of my mouth, I let out a single word, "Deal."

Stepping aside, I gestured for her to enter. "Why don't we share that cake here? I've got something that might go better with it than Medalla Light."

Her eyes sized me up, a smirk on her lips. "Oh? And what might that be?" she asked, her tone playful yet cautious.

I paused, my signature grin on full display as I caught the hint of challenge in her tone. Leaning closer, just enough to share the warmth of a whispered secret, I replied, "Never mind, I don't think you're ready for that just yet." The hint hung in the air, an indecent proposal left unspoken.

Amanda raised an eyebrow, her smirk deepening. "So I guess it's my place then? Fifteen minutes?"

"Make it twenty," I shot back, a lazy smile spreading across my face. "I want to take a shower first."

She nodded, the playful glint in her eyes remained. "Fair enough. Don't keep me waiting too long though."

Standing there, I let my gaze linger on her ass as she pranced across my lawn, crossing over to her side of the property line, her silhouette sharp against the fading light. "Neighbor pussy?," I muttered to myself.

I felt the tug of my smirk.

Heading back inside, I couldn't shake off the lustful atmosphere that hung in the air like the aftertaste of a strong shot. In the shower, my dick was half hard, and the hot water pounded across my body, racing down my thighs, and the pulse of anticipation throbbed in my veins.

Just before wrapping a towel around my waist, I peeped at my naked reflection in the mirror—grinning. "Let's see what you got, Amanda," I said aloud, a challenge thrown to my sexy reflection. I threw on some clothes that were giving casual, but sharp—no need to look like I tried too hard.

Grabbing my keys, I stepped out of my house. The night air was warm as I stepped onto the concrete pathway and later into the grass Amanda had just walked. The soft crunch underfoot marked each step toward what promised to be an interesting evening.

What did Amanda have planned with that cold Medalla Light, and what might follow? Most importantly, how far was I willing to let this go? The walk was short, but each step ramped up my anticipation.

I approached her door; tonight was about fun, about exploring whatever playful challenge Amanda was set to throw my way.

Taking a deep breath, I prepared to dive into whatever lay ahead; the secrets of the night were about to unfold.

CHAPTER EIGHT

FLIRTING WITH SECRETS

The soft hum of casual conversation enveloped us in my cozy lounge, the red walls casting a warm, embracing hue over the room. Santé cradled a half-empty Medalla Light, his muscular frame relaxed on my plush red leather couch. I gently swirled my Liquid Light Rosé wine a few times before allowing my fingers idly to trace the stem of my wineglass; intermittently, I looked at Santé's prominent outline of his manhood showing through his gray sweat shorts.

Trying to maintain a professional demeanor, I steered our dialogue towards more neutral topics, even as my mind occasionally wandered to less innocent thoughts. "So, this one time, I climbed Mauna Kea," I began, my voice filled with deliberate pauses, "The sunset, Santé, it was like the universe revealing its soul, painting colors I had never seen before across the vast expanse."

Internally, a chuckle bubbled up at my embellishment. *Okay, Amanda, maybe the universe's soul is a touch too much.* Still, Santé seemed captivated, his eyes reflecting the colors of my exaggerated sunset, which I noticed when I released a soft sigh of contentment.

Santé met my tale with one of his own, recounting a basketball game where he'd scored the winning point from a seemingly impossible shot. "I eyed that hoop, Manda," he said, his voice thick with nostalgia, "from way out on the three-point line, with the clock ticking down. I sent up a prayer with that ball, and swish—right into the basket. The crowd erupted."

I offered a playful smirk; the intellectual challenge of sparring with Santé was invigorating. "Divine intervention on the basketball court?" His story, likely embellished as well, mirrored the playful dance of our conversation.

He laughed, a rich, hearty sound that filled the room. "Perhaps! Or just dumb luck, but let's go with your divine intervention idea."

For the next half hour, our conversation meandered through topics, each laced with undertones of flirtation. Every word Santé said seemed to carry a double meaning, and I found myself caught between my professional demeanor and the growing attraction I felt towards him.

The dangers of getting too close, of letting personal feelings cloud my judgment, were clear. Yet, as a woman increasingly fascinated by the enigma that was Santé Sabatino, I could not help but probe deeper. My intellectual and personal curiosity burned bright, urging me to unravel the man before me.

I was relieved, albeit momentarily, when the phone call I had been expecting finally arrived. The ringtone sliced through the air between our sentences. I excused myself to answer the call from the other side of the room. Although I knew who it was, I still glanced at the caller ID—Isaac. There was a moment's hesitation, then I answered, mindful that Santé's curious eyes lingered on me.

"Hey, 'I'... No, it's okay... But I'll have to call you a bit later, I have company. Yes, I'm new to the area, and my attractive neighbor is here, and I was just getting to know him... I promise, I'll call you back later, okay? I promise, I'll be all ears. Yeah, talk soon."

Returning to my seat, I explained, almost apologetically, "One of the curses of people knowing I used to be a therapist is that they always call me for advice."

Santé's curiosity sharpened. "So you're a therapist? How long have you been doing that?"

I smirked, brushing a curl from my cheek. "I was... a therapist," I said, letting the word linger. "I've transitioned to consulting work now—HR for companies, helping them manage employees. It's comfortable remote work, and much less... personal."

His shoulders relaxed slightly, and his tone turned casual. "So you don't see clients anymore?"

I shook my head as I lied. "Not for a while now. I much prefer the corporate side of things."

He leaned in slightly, adopting a quasi-serious tone. "Okay, let's get to the truth."

My heart skipped a beat, a small knot forming in my stomach. "The truth about what?"

His grin widened, warm and disarming. "Were you telling the truth when you told your friend on the phone that you thought I was attractive?"

Relief washed over me, unclenching the tension in my chest. "Yeah, I told the truth," I admitted, my cheeks warming. "But I probably shouldn't have said that."

"Why not?" His tone was playful, but his eyes held a deeper curiosity.

I hesitated. "Because we don't know each other that well... not yet."

He nodded slowly, his gaze both intense and gentle. "Precisely... not yet."

A blush crept up the side of my face, and I sipped my wine to hide it. He added, his voice low and conspiratorial, "Don't worry—it'll just be our secret."

The irony wasn't lost on me, and I couldn't help but smile at the thought of Santé acknowledging the exchange of secrets—Santé's Secrets.

CHAPTER NINE

FREAKY FOR FIVE

Forty-five minutes passed like a belch; I barely noticed the back-and-forth of our conversation. Amanda, with her sneaky eyes sizing up my dick, and the easy conversation, made for a warm environment. Her lounge was hype; it had red walls, but it still felt like a comforting space where we could keep shit real.

"I complain about it sometimes," Amanda confessed, her cherry-brown eyes as soft as the gentle light of the room. "But I like being that listening ear. My friends know they can talk to me about anything. No matter how provocative, I'm a safe space." She leaned back, a slight smirk on her lips, "Besides, I think I've heard it all at this point."

My light chuckle escaped just before I said, "I'm willing to bet you've never heard anything quite like my wild escapades, Manda."

To my surprise, Amanda called my bluff; she rose gracefully, her sexy phat ass sauntering over to her purse. She pulled out a five-dollar bill, laying it dramatically on the glass coffee table in front of us, like a scene from a flick. "Surprise me," she challenged, with a playful spark in her eye.

A strange comfort pulsed through me, a rare feeling, particularly when sharing stories of my life with a woman. My stories had been strictly for the fellas, where I was assured no judgment; in fact, my smut stories earned me mad respect among most men.

A woman? I wasn't completely convinced she could handle my freak stories, but I certainly wanted to give her the opportunity.

I told her about my most recent time with Holly, the blowjob in the dugout. Yet, I twisted the tale ever so slightly to appear more mutually beneficial, to appeal to my audience of one.

Halfway through the story, Amanda interrupted, "Wait, I'm sorry to stop you but are you telling me that during halftime, while her boyfriend was inside waiting for you to return to the court, you were in the dugout, behind the basketball building, intertwined in a sixty-nine with his girlfriend?"

I smiled. "I'm not saying he was waiting for me specifically, but he was a fan of mine. Just turns out, his chick was a better fan of mine." I watched Amanda's face closely for the slightest hint of disapproval. To my surprise, she seemed intrigued. I thought she might just be the newest freak I needed in my life.

Amanda's lack of judgment inspired a confession: "I swear I would have fucked her good, but I just didn't have enough time." Amanda replied with an astonished "Wow." But then she asked a question I wasn't prepared to answer: "So when did all of this happen?"

As much as I wanted to keep it completely real, there was no way I would tell Amanda the truth and reveal that my freak session with Holly had occurred last night. Instead, I lied, saying, "Oh, that was a few years ago. I've been a little calmer recently. But I have lots of stories about my past."

Amanda chuckled and said, "Well, I guess I'll have to invite you over more often."

At first, I couldn't tell if she was serious, but the look on her face couldn't hide her enjoyment; she really got off on the stories. I didn't think she actually came, but I was pretty sure her pussy was wet.

When I stopped speaking, Amanda simply leaned back, eyes wide but not quite shocked. She slid the five dollars back toward me. "You can keep this," she said, seemingly amused and with a hint of something deeper, perhaps intrigue; she continued, "That might be the best story I've heard in a very long time. It was… provocative and risqué, to say the least."

I could feel the night coming to a close, so I excused myself teasingly, I said, "I have an early rise for my commute. Not all of us have the luxury of working from home."

Amanda smiled bashfully before walking me to her front door. I reached for her extended hand and gently kissed it. Since I had been a freak all evening, I wanted to show her I could pull off being a gentleman too, especially while I was in pursuit.

She said, "Thank you for a lovely evening, *Mr.* Santé."

It was my turn to blush slightly as I gracefully made my exit.

After offering respectful parting words, I maintained my silence on the outside, while my inner thoughts swirled, begging the larger question: Was I actually in the pursuit? Internal dialogue swirled through my mind. Maybe I should make Manda mine? Or at least put her on the roster. As I walked back across our lawns, I considered future possibilities—while groping my dick.

CHAPTER TEN

THE WAITING GAME

I knew I wasn't dreaming, but I wasn't fully awake either. That smell of old wood and musty carpet meant I was back in that small, cramped apartment in North Philly. Sixteen again, sitting on the edge of my bed, dreading the ass-whoopin' that was coming.

I'd been in another fight—this time it wasn't at school but in the neighborhood. I won, of course; my knuckles were still sore from the hits I'd landed, and my heart was still pumping with leftover adrenaline. I could hear the city's faint noises outside my window, a reminder that the world kept moving while mine had hit pause.

"Get to your room," my mom Lydia had said, her voice cold as ice. "Wait there." Lydia's punishments were legendary. She didn't believe in quick, hot-tempered payback. Nah, she made you wait. And waiting was the worst part.

From 3:45 P.M., until 11:45 P.M., I sat in that small room on the second floor. The sun had set outside the small window long ago; looking out onto busy East Allegheny Avenue, the room was even darker than earlier. No food, no communication, no clue when the punishment would start or end. Every minute dragged on, torturous in its uncertainty.

I learned a valuable lesson in those hours. The waiting, the anticipation—it was more effective than any immediate punishment. It was psychological warfare, and Lydia was a master. She knew how to make the punishment linger in your mind, festering, building anxiety and dread.

Finally, at 11:45 P.M., just as I was taking off my faded acid-washed jeans and yellow and white shirt, the door creaked open. My mom stood there, long belt strap in hand, framed by the dim hallway light. Without a word, she delivered the tremendous ass-whoopin' I'd been dreading. Ass-wacks bounced off the walls for at least thirty minutes. Lydia's outburst of violence did little to quiet my rage; in fact, it only made my anger stronger.

Two days later, with testosterone making my dick wake up two hours before me and causing my muscles to ache for battle, I decided to channel my aggression differently.

I found and joined a boxing gym. The moment I walked in, I felt a shift. The smell of leather, the mighty thud of gloves hitting bags, the grunts of effort—it felt like home. Boxing became my outlet, a way to focus my anger and frustration into something productive.

It was my fifth visit to the boxing gym when I got the last phone call from my father, Eduardo Sabatino. He and Lydia had officially separated two years prior, and his visits had become lazy. I never expected much from him, certainly not since my mom had been bad-mouthing me for weeks, even though I was doing better in school.

"Hey, Santé," his voice crackled through the phone line. There was a pause, like he wasn't sure what to say next. "I heard about your grades improving."

I was surprised. This wasn't the conversation I'd anticipated. "Yeah," I replied cautiously, wondering where this was going.

"Your mother told me about the boxing too. That's good. It's good to have a focus for all that—energy."

For a moment, I felt a flicker of something—pride, maybe. "Thanks, Dad."

Dad told me, "Don't waste your time on anger. Find something you're passionate about and go after it with everything you've got. He breathed deeply and added, "Life is short, son." His tone suddenly became serious. "Live it to the fullest." I promised I would, and we ended the call.

Those were the last words I heard from my father. Two weeks later, he was killed in an automobile accident. His advice danced in the air long after the call ended and had a weight and significance that I couldn't have understood at the time.

After his death, his words stuck with me. Boxing became more than just a way to manage my aggression. It became a passion, a purpose. Later, I added basketball to my competitive roster.

With both sports, I learned to endure, to wait out the worst of it, and to come out stronger on the other side. Lydia's punishments and Eduardo's infrequent, but cherished words of encouragement shaped me in ways I didn't fully understand until much later.

I remember sitting on that tiny bed in North Philly, my eyes red from the tears after learning of my father's passing; surrounded by wood paneling and the sounds of a bustling city outside, I learned the value of patience and focus. Life threw punches, and I learned to punch back, but with purpose, with control.

The lessons of my past—the pain and the waiting—became the foundation of who I was to become. A man who understood that true strength wasn't in the immediate retaliation but in the calculated, measured response. A man who knew that sometimes, the greatest punishment was making someone wait, making them live with anxiety and the fear. Just like Lydia taught me.

Back fully in the present, as I lay in the dark of my bedroom, I rose to take a quick nighttime piss. Holding my dick for the perfect aim, I knew that I had found a way to survive through the tough times and even managed to thrive. Returning to bed for the last few hours of sleep before I had to rise, I was confident I would always find my own path, my own way to live life to the fullest, just as my father had advised.

*She fell into his eyes like deep water—
by the time she surfaced, she was already on her knees.*

CHAPTER ELEVEN

LOCKER ROOM HERO

"So, I was digging into this bitch's pussy hard; I was at least nine inches deep; her ass cheeks were clapping around my dick so fast, it sounded like a round of applause in that motherfucker." It was Monday morning, and my story mesmerized all the men in the locker room; a few newbies didn't even look like they were breathing. That's when I turned up the suspense. "Then all of a sudden, her man starts banging on the front door."

Gasps filled the locker room.

Brian asked, "Yo, he actually came back to the house?"

I said, "Yup."

José replied, "Dead-ass? Did he know you were in the closet from earlier?"

I replied, "I doubt it."

The young boi, Fred, said, "Fuck all dat, What-chew do?"

I ground my hips behind an imaginary woman and said, "I fucked that bitch even harder."

As I boasted, laughs, giggles and high-fives broke out among the all-male crew. I had them captivated, so I continued. "She tried to scream into a pillow, but I pulled her hair like this..." I pantomimed, pulling the hair of the imaginary girl in front of me. At the same time, my hip thrust became more powerful and increased speed.

"Daaaamn, you'se a bold motherfucker." remarked José.

I replied, "For sure."

Paul asked. "I know he left his keys in the house, but what if he had found another pair? Did you think about that?"

"Nope," I said confidently, "I was just concerned with getting my nut. So I put my foot right in the center of Sheila's back, keeping her face down and ass up. That's when she sprung a leak."

José yelled, "She's a squirter... Sheila's a squirter?"

"I can't talk about how she is with other motherfuckers." I replied, then said, "All I know is that bitch couldn't stop squirting all over 'my' dick."

Paul turned to José and asked, "You know his Sheila?

I said, "Jose and Fred know her; she used to work with us at my old job."

Fred added, "That's where he met Kay, too."

Paul asked, "Kay from payroll upstairs?"

José replied, "The one and only."

Paul managed to mutter an amazed "Wow."

Brian chimed in, "One smut story at a time. Finish the story about Sheila; we're gonna be late getting on the floor."

Just at that moment, Lee walked into the locker room with annoyance. "You guys are already late to be on the floor, and now I know why."

That old motherfucker looked directly at me. Inside I thought, *If we were on the streets, I'd crack his fucking jaw.* But since my gig was worth more to me than the sweet but brief satisfaction of whooping his ass, I simply said, "Sup, Lee?"

Lee said, "Trying to work with my team, but you've got them caught up in story-time."

I wasn't gonna let him slide. "Your team?" I asked.

Paul naïvely asked, "Wait, you got the shop supervisor's position?"

A hush fell over the room. The raunchy camaraderie was replaced with tension, and I hated it.

I said, "Nawh, that can't be right. Joel told me there are a few candidates for the position, and I'm one of them." I stuffed my phone and other belongings into my locker.

Lee chuckled. "You?" He asked with a snarl.

I slammed my locker door. "Yeah, me, what about it?"

Fred said, "Yo, everybody just chill for a minute."

I replied, "Oh, I'm chill. I'm chill as fuck. It's Lee who came in here with a chip on his fuckin shoulder."

Lee backed down, saying, "No, Santé, I don't have a chip anywhere; I just want us to get on the floor because we have quotas to make, and we can't do that here in the locker rooms."

My homie Brian said, "We can get to the quotas in a minute. How did it end with Sheila? Did you get to bust ya nut? Does the bitch swallow? Come on, you can't leave us hanging."

Fred added, "Facts!" Then asked, "Did homie get back into his house? What happened?"

I decided to take my frustration out on the fellas and make Lee the focus of their anger.

I said, "Well, since your self-appointed team leader, Lee, says we have to get to the shop floor—now, I'll give you the abbreviated version."

Most of the fellas looked disappointed; Lee appeared irritated, but I wrapped up my story.

I said, "After about another ten minutes, I came on the bitch's face and darted out the back door."

The fellas let out hoots of approval, a few slow clapped.

José asked, "Do you think dude ever knew you were in there fucking his girl?"

"For sure," I replied confidently.

Fred asked, "How can you be so certain? I thought you said he never saw you?"

I explained, "He didn't see me, but I know he saw my underwear."

Laughter erupted, and Paul asked, "How do you know he saw your underwear?"

A broad smile filled my face as I said, "Because when Sheila went to the door to make sure the coast was clear, I wiped my dick off with my underwear and slipped them in what was clearly his sock drawer."

Gasps once again filled the room, and I strolled to the locker room exit, looked back, and said, "Then I slid my gray sweats on and darted out the back door. See you, motherfuckers, on the floor."

I left the fellas amused and amazed, and at least one of them totally annoyed.

*She fell into his eyes like deep water—
by the time she surfaced, she was already on her knees.*

CHAPTER TWELVE

BOUNCE AND BACKUP PLAN

It was Tuesday morning, and I took the stairs two at a time; my mind was thumping with thoughts and what-ifs. I felt a pounding pulse of anticipation and worry with each step. I won't lie; the freedom the divorce gave me was a sweet escape, even with the bitter financial pill I had to swallow. I had fewer mouths to feed at home, but between Jackie asking for money, child support, and that damn mortgage, I needed a come-up. The shop supervisor title at Manning & Mercer Containers and the raise that came with that new position were just what I needed.

As a young Puerto Rican boy from the badlands of Philly who had his scrapes with the law, I had made it much further than much of my family, friends, and old-school teachers thought I would, But I still wanted more for my life.

How could I do better than owning a five-bedroom house in New Jersey and a paid-off vehicle? How about owning a few investment properties and a side hustle with little or no debt? The shop manager position and the increased pay would go a long way in making my goals a reality. So, I made sure to put my best foot forward.

I looked at Elaine, the central office secretary. Her blue blouse showing off those ancient tits was a touch too much, but her tone soothed me; her gentle, maternal voice, "Santé, he won't be long. Head on back; he knows you're waiting. Kay is the only one in the back offices, so you won't be disturbing anyone."

Elaine's tip-off that Joel was at his car spun my wheels for a moment. I made sure to show up early to show that I was serious about this, and Joel was outside playing in his car. What the fuck? My jaw tightened, annoyed, but nawh, I wouldn't let Joel's disregard throw me off. Eyes on the prize, Santé.

I took the journey alone through the back offices; all that emptiness felt weird, a strange sight, without the usual hustle and bustle. When I reached Kay, it took her a while before she would finally acknowledge me, and even then, it was with the briefest flicker of her eyes from her screen. "Pssst…Hey." I said, trying to snap her out of whatever she was doing that was more important than me.

Her fingers danced rapidly over the keys, her expression twisted in focus. I tried to keep myself from cursing her the fuck out. I said, "What's going on with you?" "I see you, Papito," she replied, without looking up, "just finishing this blog entry."

My frustration bubbled. Kay was the payroll manager, not the blog manager. Still, keeping my cool was the priority. I said, "Got my interview with Joel soon. Wish me luck." Kay perked up, finally giving me the attention I deserved.

As she bounced over to me, I remembered why I had been fucking her for almost ten years. She had sexy, round, natural tits and was the most slutty of all my bitches. Victoria was the most submissive and gave the best head, but Kay would do anything, and I mean anything, as far as sex was concerned.

I had just fucked Kay in Joel's office yesterday on the low while he was in Pittsburgh, but even so, laying eyes on her, I wanted another go. I remembered her bright pink tongue swiping my creamy beige balls while the click of Joel's office door was still in the air.

I also remembered fucking her up against the office wall and how I would have shoved my dick up her ass had we had more time. But getting enough time in Joel's office, just the two of us, was rare. One day, I planned to find a time when Joel and everyone else was away—a moment I could take my time and enjoy an all-access pass into each of her holes. But the timing had to be right, so I had to wait.

Kay, like most of my top roster bitches, was older than me. Kay was also a few years older than my ex-wife Jackie, too. She was an M.I.L.F. in her mid-forties, divorced with a little girl—Kay was super cool. She was also a white woman who liked her man-meat with some color.

We first started fucking around at my first welding job; back then, she was the one who was married, and Jackie and I were just dating. When Kay got divorced, I got married. Kay, Victoria, and most women wanted to trap me into marriage, but Jackie was the only one that finally bagged me.

I only did the marriage thing because Jackie found the emails from Victoria, Kay, and about six other lower-roster bitches. I had to go big to save my family; for Jackie, that meant marriage.

Thinking back, it's hard for me to believe I actually gave up all of my best hoes for almost two years. After the two-year mark, I returned to creeping. But the best time by far was after my divorce. I could fuck whoever I wanted again, and that included Kay, the five-foot-six freaky down-for-whatever slut.

As Kay made her way over to me, her long curly brown hair bounced up and down in combination with her tits. Her big brown eyes were wide and cheerful; she smiled like a teenager despite her real age.

Kay gave me a big hug and sealed it with a soft kiss. "Good luck, babe, I'm here for you," her smile, sweet and seemingly genuine, swept across her face. When I tested her sincerity, "Do you mean that? Are you really here for me?"

Kay's reply was swift. "Of course I mean it," she said. I pecked her cheek in return. "Good, I might need you as 'Plan B' if this meeting doesn't pan out." Kay looked at me with a mix of confusion and passion. I could tell from her puzzled look Kay had no idea what I had in mind, but I knew I had a secret backup plan. I was determined to get my promotion—by any means necessary.

*She fell into his eyes like deep water—
by the time she surfaced, she was already on her knees.*

CHAPTER THIRTEEN

PIECES IN PLAY

Joel's office was a trip. Six Jenga towers scattered strategically over the mid-sized room, looking like a kid was in charge. One particularly large Jenga tower was stacked on the cabinet in the corner of his office, and another large one was on his desk, looking fragile as fuck.

An old game boy and a Rubik's cube also lay near the edge of his desk next to his big, old, clunky desktop computer with a swivel screen. Joel was one weird dude.

Out of strategic curiosity, I slid open his desk drawer; nothing exciting caught my eye. Then I opened the top drawer of his black cabinet, revealing a stash of employee performance reviews. My heart raced as I hunted for mine.

I straight up panicked when I heard footsteps approaching in the hall. Assuming it was Joel, I carefully shut the cabinet, making sure that damn Jenga tower wouldn't fall.

Avoiding a collapse, I raced back to the chair in front of Joel's desk. I sucked in a deep breath and slowly allowed my breath to escape just as Joel entered.

What happened next could be best described as nerve-wracking formality and bizarre as fuck. Joel's fingers were working over a Rubik's Cube while we were in the middle of a serious conversation about my future.

He seemed lost in thought, meticulously working through the colorful puzzle. Yet, his voice sounded focused on business; it was downright weird.

"Santé," he began, his eyes lifting for just a second from the twisting cube, "The pandemic did a number on us, more than I ever anticipated. Laying the guys off... that was new territory for me." He sighed, one hand twisting a layer of the cube, his fingers moving with the ease mine usually did when I fingered bitches.

I offered a nod, my own memories of the layoffs flashing through my mind. Joel's eyes met mine, lingering there for a moment before his attention was called back to the scrambling colors in his fingers.

"That's why the offices look like a ghost town," he continued, a soft click-clack of the cube's movements punctuating his words. "Business ain't back to what it was."

My eyes flickered between Joel's face and his hands, which worked the cube seemingly without needing his full attention. Despite the casual fiddling, his next words were heavy and pointed.

"As you know, the shop manager position is opening up, and your name's in the hat, Santé. But I've gotta level with you." He paused, aligning the colors with swift, precise movements. "Your age and how well you know the floor crew... it could be a problem."

My brow rose as a reflex, "What's that supposed to mean, Joel?" I asked.

He halted his manipulations of the damn cube, looking at me straight. "Leadership means respect, Santé. Sometimes, being buds with the crew can muddle that respect."

My inside thought was, *"Fuck'dem Niccas."* But I kept my exterior calm, responding evenly, "Look, I might be cool with them, but, Joel, I know how to keep it professional. If I have to crack the whip, or even let someone go, I will."

Joel nodded, slowly scrambling the now-solved Rubik's Cube. It was kinda irritating, watching him mess up what he'd just fixed, only to fuck it up again, then solve it again as he continued speaking. "There's another side to this, Santé. Bonding with the crew, especially outside of work hours, is vital too."

He gave examples, talking about Lee and his little get-togethers. My insides churned at the thought of spending my precious free time with a bunch of hard-head motherfuckers on my off time. Didn't Joel know I had bitches to fuck? But I kept my poker face intact, merely replying, "Okay, thanks for the heads up."

Joel, who seemed satisfied with my response or maybe too obsessed with his fucking cube, ended the meeting with a 'promise of transparency,' "I'm gonna be going over the pre-pandemic performance reviews, thinking over leadership skills, and considering that off-hours camaraderie. That's the deal."

We stood, and as we shook hands, his eyes lifted from his freshly scrambled puzzle. He looked at me with a mysterious expression. I said, "I hope, in the end, you'll find that I'm the best man for the job."

Joel's half-smile was all I got. "Time will tell, Santé."

I left Joel's office with images of that damn cube and his fingers working overtime. Walking down the back staircase to the shop floor, I realized I had my own puzzle to solve: How could I make sure the shop supervisor position would be mine—guaranteed.

CHAPTER FOURTEEN

COLLATERAL DAMAGE

I had just settled onto the couch, about to turn on the TV, when my laptop pinged with an incoming FaceTime call. Jackie's name flashed on the screen. My heart sank, knowing this conversation wouldn't be easy. I walked from the dining room to the living room, where my laptop was opened on the small folding TV dinner table. With a sigh, I clicked to accept the call.

Jackie's face appeared, and her expression was a storm of anger. "After everything you put me through, all the infidelity, the secret lies, the double life you led, you have the nerve to object to me taking the kids for a little time away?" she demanded, her voice trembling with barely controlled rage.

I felt my blood boil, my hands clenched into fists. "Those are my children as much as yours, Jackie. You should have consulted me, especially since this so-called vacation interferes with my visitation," I said, trying to keep my voice steady.

Jackie's eyes narrowed, her voice dripping with contempt. "This isn't about the kids, is it?"

"What else would it be about, Jac?" I asked.

"It's about you trying to control me through them, and the visitation order," she shot back, her eyes blazing with defiance.

"I don't care what you do with your life, Jackie. My only concern is the kids," I replied, my throat tight with frustration and hurt.

Jackie let out a bitter laugh. "If the kids were your ultimate concern, you wouldn't have had a bevy of bitches."

I felt a sharp sting in my gut but pushed it aside. "Besides Victoria and that one last incident, you have no proof of your other allegations. But I have photographs of your fucking around on me. So don't speak as if you have the moral high ground," I retorted, my voice growing louder with each word.

Jackie's face twisted with rage. "The only reason you have that so-called proof is because your mistress hired someone to get the photos in the first place. By the way, how's your gunshot wound?" she sneered.

Her words hit me like a punch to the gut. I struggled to find a response. Before I could give her the cussing she deserved for her low blow, Santé Junior appeared in the background, waving enthusiastically.

"Hi, Dad!" he called out, his innocent voice cutting through the tension.

A warmth spread through my heart that only my children could bring. "Hey, son! I love you. Daddy's gonna see you soon," I said, forcing a smile as I felt a surge of love for my boy.

Jackie glared at me. "Don't make promises to the kids that you don't know you can keep," she snapped, her voice cold as fuck.

I felt my forehead warm, but I struggled to keep my anger under control. "I'm not doing this in front of the kids," I said through gritted teeth. Just then, Jovie, my nine-year-old daughter, joined Santé Junior, my eleven-year-old boy. Their faces lit up when they saw me, and I felt a bittersweet joy.

"Hi, Daddy!" Jovie chirped, her voice a bright spot in the tension.

"Hey, sweetie. How's the vacation?" I asked, trying to keep my voice light despite my rage and bubbling guts.

"It's fun! We went to the beach and built sandcastles," Jovie said, her eyes sparkling with excitement.

"Did you try surfing, Santé Junior?" I asked, my heart aching with each beat.

"Yeah, but I fell a lot," he said, laughing. His laughter was medicine to my soul, even if only temporarily.

I probed for more details, wanting to understand their surroundings and if there was some motherfucker lurking around my children. "Have you met any new friends? Maybe any new uncles?" I asked, watching their faces closely.

Their faces scrunched up in confusion. I heard Jackie yelp, "Ugh!" Before they could answer, Jackie cut in. "Listen, don't mind your father. He's tired and doesn't know what he's saying. It's time for dinner; go wash your hands."

As the kids started to leave the screen, Santé Junior turned back. "When will I see you, Dad?" he asked, his voice filled with hope and longing.

I felt tears sting my eyes, but I held them back. "Very soon, Papito, you'll see Daddy in two or three weeks. I promise," I said, my voice breaking slightly.

The kids walked off-screen, and Jackie returned to the center. "By the way, I need more money for Junior's clothes. He's growing like a weed," she said, her tone all businesslike and detached.

I leaned close to the screen, my voice low and intense. "I should never have loved you, bitch!"

Without waiting for her response, I popped my finger across the laptop and ended the video call. I slammed the computer shut and pushed myself back onto the couch, feeling the stress of the conversation ravage my body.

I put my hand over my eyes, demanding myself to regain control. "You're a man," I reminded myself. "Don't let that bitch make you like her. Don't get emotional and overwhelmed." I ran my hands through my hair, feeling the frustration and sadness ease but a fraction.

I reached for the TV remote and clicked it on. The 75-inch screen lit up with a basketball game already in progress. The noise and action offered a temporary escape, but despite my efforts at discipline, the ache in my heart remained.

*She fell into his eyes like deep water—
by the time she surfaced, she was already on her knees.*

CHAPTER FIFTEEN

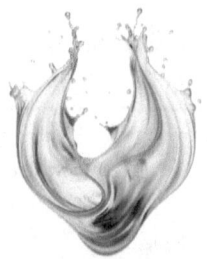

A WARNING NAMED 'J'

In the peach-toned warmth of my kitchen, I juggled the phone between my shoulder and ear as I prepared my salad. The clatter of lettuce and vegetables punctuating our conversation. Isaac's voice crackled through the phone, laced with concern. "How's it going, Amanda? Have you been able to keep your distance?"

I chuckled softly, tossing a handful of kale into the bowl. "As much as I can, but he's persistent. Texts, visits—he's always finding a way to reach out."

There was a momentary pause on the other end, and I could almost picture Isaac furrowing his brow in thought. "You know, Amanda," he finally said, his tone cautious, "you've been spending a lot of time with him lately. Are you sure you're not getting too close?"

I sighed, the weight of Isaac's words settling in the pit of my stomach. "I won't deny there's an attraction, Isaac. But I'm staying focused on our goal. We need to gather as much information as we can for the book."

Another pause, this one heavier than the last. "I just worry about you, Amanda," Isaac confessed, his voice softening. "This whole thing—it's risky. And I don't want to see you get hurt."

My fingers stilled as I listened to Isaac's words, the sincerity in his voice tugging at my heartstrings. "I appreciate your concern, Isaac," I replied, my tone gentle. "But I'm not alone in this. We're in it together, remember?"

There was a brief silence, the intensity of our shared history hanging in the air between us. "Yeah, I remember," Isaac said, his voice filled with nostalgia. "We've been through a lot, haven't we?"

I nodded, even though he couldn't see me. "We have," I agreed, a small smile playing at the corners of my lips. "And we'll get through this, too. Together."

With that, we fell into a comfortable silence, the sounds of my kitchen serving as a backdrop to our conversation as I continued to prepare my salad. I sensed a shift in Isaac's tone. "Amanda," he began tentatively, "There's something I need to tell you."

I paused mid-slice, my heart skipping a beat at the solemnity in his voice. "What is it, Isaac?" I asked softly, his words hanging heavy in the air.

There was a moment of hesitation before Isaac spoke again, his voice tinged with regret. "Six years ago today," he confessed, "May 7th 2016, was the day it happened with 'J'."

"And by 'it' you mean what, precisely?" I asked carefully.

"Girl, don't be dense." Isaac said, with annoyance brimming.

Then, in a burst of raw honesty, he blurted out, "Fine. By 'it,' I mean the first time 'J' put his dick in my mouth."

The sound of the knife slipping from my fingers and clattering against my countertop punctuated the heavy silence that accompanied my shock. Isaac's confession hung in the air between us, thick with the mix of his vulgarity and vulnerability.

"Oh, sweetheart," I said, empathy pouring from me like an overflowing cup.

Isaac said, "Quickly, it became a thing two or three times a week. No real words between us, mainly moans and groans." He added, "But I knew, he knew I loved him. I wouldn't have let him fuck me if I hadn't loved him."

Isaac attempted to break the uncomfortable tension by saying, "After all, I'm no whore."

Although I chuckled lightly, I felt a pang of sadness at the mention of Isaac's past with his infamous lover, 'J,' a flood of memories washing over him.

"How long had you been in love with 'J' before the first time?" I asked gently, knowing that this conversation was long overdue.

Isaac's response was immediate, the words tumbling out in a rush. "From the moment he walked into the audiovisual room in high school," he admitted, his voice thick with emotion. "But I was closeted back then—to my family, to my friends, to even myself. You know how I was back then."

I felt a surge of empathy as Isaac bared his soul, his hidden desires finally coming to light. "Wow. That's two decades of longing," I murmured, my heart aching for the pain he had endured. "It must have been so hard for you."

There was a pause on the line, followed by Isaac's exhale—a mix of frustration and nostalgia.

I frowned slightly. "Yeah... wait." Something clicked. "J went to high school with us? Why don't I remember him?"

The silence stretched just a little too long.

Finally, Isaac cleared his throat. "That's because we didn't actually have classes together back then. You were a senior."

I let out a short laugh. "Great way to call me old, thanks. I'm only a year older than you."

Isaac groaned. "I know. Can we get back to the point?"

I sighed, shaking my head as if he could see me. "I'm sorry... that you've been carrying a torch for him for so long."

Isaac's voice was heavy with regret. "Yeah, my secret torch," he admitted. "But it's more complicated than that, Amanda. 'J' wasn't just my secret—he was my forbidden desire."

There was a brief silence on the line before he continued. "But nothing happened between us physically... not until after 'J' got caught with his own forbidden fruit—Tammy."

I heard him exhale through the phone, his voice quieter but no less weighted. "He got busted about a year into his new marriage."

I suddenly felt like a viewer of a tawdry soap opera. I struggled to keep the web of characters straight. At the time, I didn't think Isaac's past with 'J' had anything to do with our current circumstances. But I wanted to be a good friend, and the story was juicy. With that in mind, I asked, "Wait, so when 'J' first married Melissa, the two of you were only friends?"

Isaac replied, "We acted that way, but I was in love with him, and he pretended not to notice."

I advanced the salacious storyline by asking, "Then 'J' started a sexual affair with Tammy, and you knew about it?"

Isaac's voice squealed. "Knew about it, I was his wingman. I was his excuse when he was running late getting back to his wife; sometimes, I was even his damn ride back to Melissa."

I couldn't hide my surprise. "Wait, you were having sex with 'J' while helping him have sex with women?

Isaac replied, No, Girl. 'J' and I didn't start gettin' it in until after Tammy blew up his marriage with Melissa. She told their whole story and provided secret pictures as proof." Isaac added, "Honey, his entire playhouse came crashing down. 'J' never forgave Tammy for revealing his affair to his wife."

Isaac's voice quivered. One night 'J' came over to my place crying and drinking; I remember he said, "I should shoot that bitch for fucking up my life." I told him, "Tammy is not worth losing the rest of your life to prison."

His eyes were glassy as he looked around my tiny apartment. 'J' said, "I just realized I have nowhere to lay my head." He had lost everything. I let him know he could spend the next few nights with me.

Isaac's revelation sent a shiver down my spine, a stark reminder of the risks of revealing secrets. "It sounds like things got messy," I remarked softly, trying to comprehend the tangled web of sex secrets and entanglements.

Isaac said, "Messy, ain't the word for the fuckery that followed." he told the rest of his story. "In the middle of the night, this Nicca came off my living room couch, strolled into my bedroom, and stood on my side of the bed. I heard something, so I opened my eyes and saw his shadow; child, I screamed like an ole white lady."

An involuntary snicker escaped me. I briefly hit the mute button, allowing Isaac to continue without hearing my reaction.

I turned on the light, and his dick was hard. Covered by his thin, tight, gray Hanes boxer briefs. I looked up at him and asked if he was okay. He shook his head and said. "Nawh, but you can make it better."

I leaned against my counter, forgetting all about food preparation. Isaac's homoerotic tale was sad, but still, it was captivating. I pressed the speakerphone button as Isaac continued with his sorted tale.

Isaac said, "'J' slid his underwear to his knees. His dick leaped toward me like a snake set free." Then he moved close and said, 'It's finally your turn. Take what you want.' "

Listening to Isaac's story my heart rate quickened. I took a deep, labored breath. It felt like the ambient air in my kitchen disappeared.

Isaac said, "That's how it started. That was the first of many times I sucked 'J' off. But his paranoia really kicked in after I let him fuck."

My heart skipped a beat at Isaac's words, a sense of foreboding creeping over me. "What do you mean?" I asked, my voice low and breathless.

Isaac hesitated for a moment, the silence stretching between us. "'J' fucked me a few times, stole both my heart, and soul, then broke things off with me."

"I'm sorry, Isaac," I whispered, my voice filled with empathy. "It must have been incredibly difficult for you."

Isaac's response was a heavy sigh, "It was," he admitted. "But that's not even the worst of it."

"What? What do you mean I asked?"

The phone line was quiet for a while. I turned off the speakerphone and placed my cell phone to my ear. Finally, Isaac confessed, his voice barely audible, "He came to my place one night. And he pulled a gun on me, Amanda."

The revelation hit me like a sledgehammer, my breath catching in my throat. "Isaac..." I gasped, the shock of his words reverberating through me. "You never told me he pulled a gun on you."

I held the phone tightly, waiting intensely for Isaac's response. "It was too painful to talk about," he admitted, his voice tinged with bitterness. "But 'J' made it clear, that if I ever breathed a word about our affair, I'd regret it."

With a heavy heart, my empathy reached out across the telephone line, my voice filled with compassion. "I'm so sorry, Isaac," I whispered, his confession settling over me like a sour blanket.

Isaac's voice trembled as he continued, "I appreciate that Amanda. He really scared me. That's why I never told anybody his real name. Except for you, my best friend, I never even mention him at all." He added, "It also helped that you happened to be a professional psychologist."

His words struck a chord, a profound sense of responsibility settling over me like a heavy cape. "Isaac," I whispered, my voice thick with emotion, "I'm honored that you trusted me with this."

There was a moment of silence as we both grappled with his confession and memories, the bond between us deepening with each passing moment.

Isaac's voice strengthened as he said, "But it's all in the past now. There's no point dwelling on what could have been."

Reflexively, I nodded in agreement; it didn't matter that he couldn't see me. "You're right," I said, my voice filled with determination. "We can't change the past, but we can learn from it. Lessons—that's what life is all about, and that's exactly what we're going to give our readers from the book about Santé."

There was a moment of silence as Isaac processed my words and I processed my emotions. The purpose of our shared mission beyond our personal ambitions was suddenly clarified between us.

"You're right, Amanda," he finally said, his voice laced with gratitude. "And, we're in this together, no matter what."

With renewed resolve, we continued our conversation, our voices mingling with the clatter of dishes I was arranging in my dishwasher and the refrigerator's hum. At that moment, I knew that no matter what obstacles lay ahead, Isaac and I would face them together. We were a team with the mutual goal of discovering and publishing—Santés' Secrets.

CHAPTER SIXTEEN

FIJI WATER AND FRUSTRATION

Last night, I was playing into a fantasy with Amanda, but by the next afternoon, the reality of my life was as harsh as a pile of fresh shit. Directly from work, I sat in the drab lobby of Luke Ferrera's office, tapping my Timberland boots against the slightly tattered burgundy carpet that smelled of mildew. The framed pictures of Luke on various magazine covers—Camden County Lawyers, Legal Eagle, Matrimonial Monthly—all seemed to be making fun of me.

It was downright baffling how unfair life could be. Jackie had taken the kids on vacation, leaving me alone with my thoughts, but I was still expected to pay child support on time.

It didn't seem right, but that's how it was. I leaned back, trying not to flip the fuck out in the law office lobby; the faint scent of lemon from the tea bags over at the self-service refreshments area was a reminder that I was in a professional setting—I had to keep my shit together.

I glanced around the lobby, noticing the small details; the beige walls were scuffed, and the light fixtures were old. Not quite the upscale place I thought my lawyer would be, considering the top dollar he was charging me.

The receptionist typed away at her computer, her expression blank and detached. I could hear the faint hum of the air conditioning. The low, persistent noise was the perfect background to my growing irritation.

Sitting there for ten minutes gave my mind time to wander back to the first time I met Luke at the same office building.

The anxiety I felt back then was undeniable. I'd been caught in a threesome, or what my attorney Luke called a ménage à trois.

Call it what you want; I had two bitches sucking on my dick at the same time, and that was after I ass fucked one, while the other one was eating my ass.

My fucking luck; my wife caught us right before I could bust my nut. That was when I knew Jackie was serious about the divorce.

I remembered sitting in the same chair I had sat the first time I visited. Back then I wondered if I'd ever see my children again and if I'd lose my house.

It took weeks for Luke to convince me that I'd get through it, that I wouldn't lose everything. Ironically, Victoria's misguided duplicity actually helped me document Jackie's affair, tipping the scales in my favor. Half-heartedly, I acknowledged to Luke that I was thankful for that.

The receptionist's voice broke through my walk down memory lane. "Mr. Sabatino, Attorney Ferrera will see you now," she called, snapping me back to the present.

I stood, adjusting my neon green shirt, feeling the fabric cling uncomfortably to my skin. I made my way to the tiny elevator and rode to the second floor. The dingy walls of the elevator added to my irritation.

When I reached Luke's office, I immediately noticed some upgrades from my last visit. The newer, sleek, modern decor felt noticeably different from my first visit and a dramatic difference from the lobby. Black and royal blue dominated the space, giving it an upscale, fancy feel. I remember thinking, "Now this is the office of a top dawg lawyer."

Taking my seat, I noticed Luke's large oak desk was covered with divorce actions and other legal stuff.

A desktop computer and two laptops were neatly arranged. The faint scent of markers highlighted the strangeness and awkwardness of the moment.

Luke greeted me with a nod, then grabbed a small bottle of Fiji water from his compact office refrigerator. "Water?" he offered.

I accepted the bottle but didn't open it. "Thanks, but I'm kinda not in the mood to drink," I said.

He motioned for me to sit, and I took the chair across from him. "So, what brings you in today, Santé?"

I cut straight to the point, "Jackie's violating the custody arrangement. I haven't seen my kids in a month, Luke. It's a mess."

Luke frowned. "I don't understand. You both have joint custody. Jackie has custodial custody, yes, but you have visitation rights. There's been no legal change to that order."

I sighed, frustrated. "Maybe not, but she's violating the visitation order. She took my damn kids on vacation. She says it's with her parents, but I suspect another dude is involved. The idea of another motherfucker around my children is driving me crazy."

Luke leaned back, his fingers steepled as he considered my words. "Is she preventing you from picking them up?"

Bam! The sound of me slamming the Fiji bottle on the oak desk ricocheted off the walls.

"Fuck, Luke, didn't you hear me? She took my Goddamned kids outta town on some bullshit vacation without even discussing it with me." I shifted in my seat, glancing at the framed law degree on the wall. "I'm telling you this shit is unfair, Luke. I fucking hate not knowing who's around my kids. Sometimes, it keeps me up at night."

I tried to lighten the mood. "That's why I don't like to sleep alone or sleep much at all when I get into bed." I chuckled as I added, "A lil' pussy keeps my mind off things, ya know?"

Luke didn't laugh. Instead, there was an awkward silence. Mr. Stiff Lawyer man looked down for a second, took a deep breath, and just as his eyes met mine, said, "Santé, while Jackie should've worked out the arrangements before leaving, this probably isn't enough to get a hearing. It will also take a while, the courts are notoriously slow."

Luke tapped his fingers on his desk and asked, "When are they supposed to return?"

"Another two weeks," I said, feeling a pressure on my chest.

Luke nodded, his expression thoughtful. "Just as I thought, it'll take longer than that to get a hearing. Hang in there, and stay current on your payments. What you're going through is part of the challenge of living a divorced lifestyle."

I said, "I guess... this is what I was trying to avoid. It's why I put up with Jackie's bullshit for so long. I didn't want anyone to dictate when I could and couldn't see my children. All these changes... it's just unfair."

Luke hesitated before responding. "I understand. It's a mess, but you'll get used to the arrangements. You're a soldier, Santé."

I stood up, my legs feeling like they were made of lead, a reminder of the unfairness and mess that came with once-loving Jackie. My hands balled into fists, and breathing lightly, I said, "The world will never know that I'm bothered at all."

Then I leaned in slightly across Luke's desk, my eyes locked with his, and said, "But I'll let you in on a little secret—not hearing my children's voices every morning, kills me a little inside every night."

Luke watched as I turned and left the office without saying goodbye, the Fiji water bottle left behind.

CHAPTER SEVENTEEN

CHOCOLATE AND CHLOE

It had been a solid week since I'd laid eyes on Amanda. A few quick "what's sup?" text messages but nothing more. So, with a healthy dose of curiosity, I marched to Amanda's front door with a boxed chocolate cake tucked under my arm.

I was surprised by the tingle in my fingers. I wasn't usually trippin over a chick, but standing in front of 20 Pond Drive, I felt a mix of nerves and excitement dancing in my gut as I raised a knuckle to her front door.

With a soft click, the door swung open; Amanda stood there, her warm smile a welcome sight. "Hey," she said with a simple yet inviting greeting; afterward, she stepped aside to let me into her house.

Standing in her small foyer area, I followed her lead and kept it light. "Hey," I said before offering her the cake with a bit of a tilt of my head, "This time, I brought something sweet.

Amanda's eyes flickered with a pleasant surprise and, maybe, a bit of appreciation that went beyond the dessert. She welcomed me in, and her kitchen became a stage for our subtle dance of snacking and soft words.

Amanda easily carved through the cake, its sweet scent lingering between us. I quietly pressed a five-dollar bill onto the counter. Her eyes shifted from the money to my ever-sparkling eyes, a silent question reflected in hers.

"This time, no bet," I said, my voice low and calm. "I've got a story for you, no strings."

Amanda offered a pause, then a nod. "Can it wait till we settle in?"

Our agreement came with a nonchalant lift of my shoulders. She slid me a beer. "Keep the five," Amanda added, teasing, as she led the way, the cake slices balanced delicately in her hands. "Deal," I chuckled softly, and I followed her into the red lounge.

Amanda's leather couch was as soft as I remembered, and the dim lights in her lounge set a sexy mood. Within seconds, I found myself telling her another freaky story, pretending it was an old tale from years ago, while I caressed a bottle of Medalla Light beer.

"So, there was this one time with this chick at work, named... Chloe," I began, watching Amanda's eyes flash with curious anticipation, completely oblivious that Chloe was a convenient, fake name for Kay. I continued, "We had this... thing, a secret thing, you know? And damn, it was wild."

Amanda was all in—totally absorbed. She leaned forward slightly, her eyes reflecting the flickering of a distant light as she looked at me. Her spoon was frozen mid-air, awaiting the next bite of cake, which she had momentarily forgotten.

"Chloe and I, we'd sneak off into the boss's office during lunch breaks," I continued, creating a web of half-truths. "We would fuck all over that office. I'd dick her on the desk and the boss's empty leather chair. It was like our secret garden... of forbidden fucking and sucking."

A smile, rich with mischief and memories, formed on my lips as I continued my story, "I'd yank her hair when I would fuck her from behind and tell her to arch her back so I could get deeper inside of her. She would reach for my hands and suck my fingers while I slid in and out of her wet pussy, especially when we were in the missionary position. "

Amanda's fork paused halfway to her mouth, her eyes wide; she said, "Really?"

"Yeah," I continued with a smirk. "We'd go in there, and it was like the world outside didn't exist. My dick would be hard from the time we closed my boss's office door. Just the thrill of secrecy, the knowledge of what we were doing, right under everyone's noses, and in the boss's office of all places!"

I could tell from the slight upward curve of Amanda's lips that she was feelin my story. But Amanda wasn't a dude, so I was careful how I told my tale. I had to make it more flowery. She wasn't yet one of my bitches, so I didn't want to scare her off.

"What else did you guys do?" Amanda whispered.

I chuckled, taking a sip of my beer. "Well, mostly, she sucked my dick." I quickly glanced at Amanda; she didn't look offended, so I pushed it a bit further. "I wanted to sixty-nine before fucking her, but on one special day Chloe had something else in mind."

Amanda moved to the edge of the red couch and leaned in; she asked, "Special? Like what?"

My voice was low and direct; I said, "She begged to eat my ass!"

Amanda gasped. "What?" Her eyes widened without a hint of judgment.

I continued, "Yup, most of the workers had sandwiches for lunch, Chloe ate my ass."

Amanda nervously laughed. Then, she looked down, and I could tell a bit of embarrassment was rising in her. But I moved forward with the story, anyway.

"The best part was when I fucked her on the desk. The sneaky vibe made her pussy extra wet. But not water wet, creamy wet, my favorite kind of wet. Chloe wasn't super tight, just tight enough.

Amanda leaned in closer. "And Chloe...? How did she like it?"

I could tell this was the part where Amanda expected some flowery female shit, so I said, "She loved it. Sometimes, we would find each other, intertwining fingers revealing a passion neither of us could voice. The moans, the fevered pace, all pushed by lust and fear.

Amanda's eyes, unblinkingly, absorbed all the bullshit; her spoon was abandoned on the plate; her full attention was an energy I could feel in the room.

I could tell a touch of careful honesty was due, so I said, "That girl... Chloe, she'd get lost in my eyes, Amanda. I saw how she melted under my gaze and crumbled under my touch. I knew she was falling; I also knew she was sinking deeper than I was."

"But I won't lie to you, Amanda," I continued, feeling a strange mix of sincerity and deceit weaving through my story. "I was hooked too, not to her; no, but to the secrecy, to the thrill, to the freaky boldness of it all. Kay—I mean Chloe's gaze offered something... reckless, and I dived into it, but I knew it was a depth I'd never allow myself to drown in."

A soft sigh whispered through the room, and Amanda's eyes held a twinge of something emotional, perhaps mirrored reflections of hidden stories of her own.

"That story, it sounds like a passion from another lifetime," Amanda whispered, the words barely crossing the edge of her lips.

Setting my beer down, I met Amanda's eyes with a gentle certainty. "That's exactly what it felt like, Manda."

As we sat there in the delicate aftermath of my revealed secrets and crafted lies, I sensed a unique thread of closeness weaving through the silence between us.

I took another swig of my beer. Amanda's eyes left mine, yet I could tell she was hooked. The atmosphere between us grew electric, and the remnants of my story stayed in the air.

A few minutes later, I saw the night pressed against Amanda's windows, then noticed the cake was nothing more than a few stray crumbs. I said, "Wow, where did the time go? I thought I'd only bother you for a few minutes."

Amanda clutched a thin silver chain around her neck and inhaled deeply. "No, you didn't bother me. The time did move pretty quickly, but you also have to consider you arrived a little after seven, so we started late." She smiled and noted, "Well, late for a school night."

I snickered, "Wow, I hadn't heard that phrase in a long while. For a micro-second, I missed my married life with Jackie. Putting the kids to bed. Lights out promptly at 8 P.M.

I quickly swallowed my emotions like a man. I stood, masking any sign of sadness by saying, "Well, I don't have school in the morning, but I do have to get up at 4:30 to head to the shop."

Amanda rose from the couch and remarked, "I know all about your interesting lunch breaks, but you never told me exactly what you do."

I was tempted to lie, but I didn't have an exciting cover story, especially one I would remember, so I told Amanda the truth, "I'm a welder. I weld shipping containers, and we start pretty early every morning."

Amanda seemed content. "That's a pretty good profession. Good money and decent security. Just another thing that makes you a good catch, I guess."

I let her flirtation linger. I knew I had to leave before I ended up fucking her right there on her leather couch in that bright red lounge of hers. So, I simply smiled and made no mention of her comment.

"Maybe we can do this again sometime," I said, strolling toward the room's exit.

Amanda followed behind me, saying. "I'd like that. Let's keep in touch. I like your text messages, especially those with your naughty stories."

I entered her small hallway thinking, "Ah, this bitch doesn't know what she's asking for." I knew my text game was tight. Plus, I really loved sexting. But I played it cool. I simply replied, "I got you."

At the doorway, Amanda gave me a soft kiss on my cheek. It lingered as a sweet end to the evening. "This felt almost like a date," she whispered her words, a tantalizing tease.

As I entered the night, her scent of gardenia, the taste of chocolate cake, and the echo of what might have been swirled around me. I found myself caught up, pondering friendship, blurred lines, and the many freaky possibilities.

*She fell into his eyes like deep water—
by the time she surfaced, she was already on her knees.*

CHAPTER EIGHTEEN

FROM PLAYS TO PLEASURES

My hand itched with the need to smack the shit out of Lee for trying to fuck up my Wednesday as he had days earlier in the week. What a fucking asshole, deciding he had some kinda right to interrupt my smut story.

Lee, the stupid fuck that appointed himself the voice of the people or whatever he called himself doing, told me some of the guys at the job might be feeling a bit uneasy with my smut stories.

"No, Nicca, it's you that's uneasy," I spat back, eyes locked onto his, "Because you ain't getting any pussy." Like the predictable coward he was, Lee backed down and shuffled out of the locker room and onto the shop floor, pussy between his legs. That was my Wednesday.

Fast forward to Friday, on the basketball court, and I found myself again battling the urge to slap the shit outta a motherfucka. This time, it was Jordan. I thought, *Man, I was the star of the Turn-*

ersville Titans, wasn't I? So, what the hell was he doing? Hogging the ball, refusing to pass it to me, trying to steal my damn shine?

Coach Richards' whistle pierced the tension at the right moment, saving Jordan's jaw. Glancing around, I could see the nervous look written all over the team's faces; They probably thought there was gonna be a beat-down back in the locker rooms. Though the thought did pass my mind a few times, I had bigger fish to fry.

As the team headed off to the locker rooms, their chatter was dull in the distance. I stayed back, my eyes pouring through the stands, scanning for smuts to add to my roster. Sam threw me a look, "Yo, you alright? He asked.

"I'm straight, go ahead," I said, nodding toward the locker room.

Once alone, my fingers fumbled for my phone, quickly firing off a message: "Where the hell is my threesome you promised?"

I wiped the last bit of sweat from my forehead as I waited for Maya's reply. She was twenty-four, so I figured she would be glued to her device like the rest of her generation. I wouldn't have been surprised if she texted while in surgery or something.

Thinking back to the fucking I gave her after a game, the connection, the heat, the promise in her eyes, I knew she'd respond soon enough. So I wasn't surprised when she pinged back a message within two minutes:

> "Me and My girlfriend I was telling you about will meet you at the motel in about three hours."

I replied with only one word, *Cool.*

And with that, my mind shifted from frustration to double fucking. I was ready to leave the basketball court and dive into some wet and ready pussies.

She fell into his eyes like deep water—
by the time she surfaced, she was already on her knees.

CHAPTER NINETEEN

TWO WAITING, ONE READY

Friday 7:35 P.M., and the neon sign sputtered, flashing like a sleazy dare—perfect for the rundown motel. The place looked like it had stories—most of them messy. My phone lit up, cutting through the darkness inside my truck.

The text message was clear, direct, and pulsing with penetrating promises:

Room 105. We're already naked Daddy.

I took a moment, glancing at myself in the rearview mirror. I looked good, I had to admit. I knew my amber-green eyes would be hard to resist. My magical eyes always had a hypnotic effect, but that night, they gave a ready-for-anything kind of gleam.

But it wasn't just the extra red hue near my pupils that would ensure wet pussies. My skin was flawless; I looked at least five years younger than my age. I gave myself a nod of approval. The bitches waiting for me were mine to conquer.

The motel was a rundown piece of shit building with paint peeling in all the right places, giving it just the right amount of raunch. I stepped out of the truck, the gravel crunching beneath my boots.

As I approached room 105, my excitement grew with each step. My knuckles lightly tapped against the door, barely breaking the thick quiet of the night. The only consistent sound was the distant traffic from the Black Horse Pike, which ran on the other side of the building.

I could hear the soft murmuring of voices inside the motel room, the female whispers shushed in anticipation. "Come in," a soft voice said. After a closer look, I noticed the door opened a crack. My lips curled into a slow smile as I entered the room.

Two steps into the place, and the scent of pussy was everywhere. The smell of pre-game sex mingled with the musty odor that seemed to always live in motel rooms was undeniable. I closed the door behind me and secured the night latch.

Maya and Bella were on a king-sized bed in the center of the room. Before me were two of my top roster bitches, naked and intertwined, waiting for me—'Big Dick Papi.' Their intentions were as clear as the shiny lip gloss on Maya's lips; they wanted to get fucked, and I was just the man for the job.

"Y'all bitches ready to work tonight?" I asked, my voice low, steady, carrying a dominating enough bite to make them sit up straight.

Maya tilted her head, her smile widening. Bella licked her lips, her gaze dropping for half a second before snapping back up at me. The smuts spoke together as one blended voice: "Yes, Papi, we're ready."

*She fell into his eyes like deep water—
by the time she surfaced, she was already on her knees.*

CHAPTER TWENTY

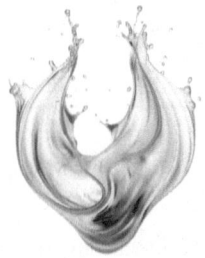

THREE UNDER THE SURFACE

My empty balls were dripping wet from the familiar warm water that first ran down my chest. My soothed, huge, tired dick hung freely. The small showerhead rained down on me, while the smell of chlorine from the pool blended into my usual routine—the one that always ended with a good, cleansing swim.

It was technically the early hours of Saturday, and the Clearwaters Swim Club was dark and private. Carol, the club's manager, had left me alone in the building. In fact, she opened the club just for me, for my after-midnight swim.

As usual, Carol wanted to suck my dick before she returned to her husband and kids, but I took a rain check. I was tired from my threesome, and I believed it was always a good idea to keep my long-term bitches hungry. So after Carol showed me how to lock the Swim Club's door, I slapped her on the ass and told her she could suck on my Puerto Rican balls another time. Carol's playful giggle echoed as she left me in peace and I returned my attention to the water.

I always loved the look of the untouched surface of the pool. As usual, I wiggled my toes against the tile underneath me, sucked in a breath, and jumped in the pool with force. The bubbles and sounds felt so familiar and soothing.

My muscles stretched across the water, the power laps, my fingers tapping the wall at each end of the pool. Then, that familiar slip happened. My body felt distant. My mind's eye kicked in, lighting up with images.

In a flash, I saw myself standing inside the motel room door with a hard dick and sweaty balls, fresh from basketball practice. Maya, my white honey, I'd been fucking off and on for five years, had a thick booty, a small gut, and huge tits. She also sported a hood attitude, which made her even hotter. "Hey, Daddy." She said, laying back on the bed while this freak-ass Mexican chick, Bella, was already eating her pussy.

Bella's ass was up and facing me. Her ass wasn't as big as Maya's but was more round. Bella spoke to me, but I couldn't understand what she said because her face was wedged between Maya's thighs. I had two flavors of pussy in front of me, and I loved it.

I quickly got naked, tossing my clothes to either side of me before reaching the bed. I was finally having the moment I had asked for and waited six months to experience.

I was huffing and blowing air out of my mouth on my third lap when the image of me jerking my large tool at the edge of the bed filled my vision. After a few moments, both chicks crawled toward me across the dingy, dull-white sheets. They rose and began sucking on my nipples; it was a real turn-on.

After a few seconds, I saw another image: Mya rubbing my dick with her small soft hands, only emphasizing my eleven inches. Glancing down at the sight made both my dick and ego grow even larger. "Suck it," I said just above a whisper.

Maya sucked the head of my dick. Her lips were warm and soft. Without saying a word, Bella joined Maya, but instead of fighting over the head of my dick, Bella lowered herself and got busy with my sweaty balls. She licked them gently at first.

I reared my head back from the pleasure but quickly looked down. I saw Bella's face; no reaction to my heavy musk. That bitch was a pro; sweaty balls were nothing new to her; she didn't even flinch. Bella was 'a real one'.

My attention drifted over to Maya and her smiling eyes as she ran her tongue around my dick's head.

As the pool's water drew me further into a trance, I remember thinking, This was the perfect way to spend a Friday evening. My mind's eye flashed to Maya playfully suggesting to Bella, "Let's switch." Maya's mouth was across my balls, and Bella sucked my dick. Unlike Maya, Bella tried to deep-throat me. I felt the head of my dick reach her tonsils when her gag reflex kicked in. She choked, I smiled; they sucked; I moaned—a good time was had by all.

Spontaneously, I found myself doing the backstroke; the water was on my back, and I was trying something new. Much like hours before, when Bella asked me to sit on her face while Maya continued to suck my dick, new, exciting, and increasingly freaky.

Bella's tongue licked my asshole with the flicker of a professional whore. I can't remember when my ass fetish began, but it's a real thing with me. I think anal sex of all types is linked to power as much as it is about pure sexual pleasure.

My arms were getting tired, but then I thought about the energy I had just expended at the motel, I got a burst of energy in the water. Vivid images of the motel freakiness played like an internal porno movie, but it was better because it was real.

I saw myself at the edge of the bed fucking Maya with slow circular strokes while Bella was kneeling behind me licking my ass; she just couldn't get enough of my flavor. Gradually, my pace increased, which gave both smuts a challenge. Maya struggled to take all of my dick inside of her pussy. At the same time, Bella tried to follow the pace of my hips while hungrily eating my ass and occasionally drifting down to lick my balls.

I knew that moment in room 105 was a special occasion, and I wanted those freaks to remember me. I had to show them who owned them. So I pushed those bitches to their sexual limits, hoping to cross over into fresh taboos.

It was time for me to fuck Bella. I sat on the edge of the bed and let her ride me. Her pussy was deep, wet, soft, and warm. She could take at least nine and a half inches of my eleven-inch dick without much struggle. Still, when I pushed her down by her shoulders, her stretching pussy made her sopping wet.

Maya was on her knees in front of us, sucking my balls. I suspected Maya could taste Bella's pussy juice because I could feel it rolling down the shaft of my dick and onto the top of my balls.

It was time to push the envelope of freakiness more. "Maya, take my dick outta her pussy and suck it." I said, my voice steady. Maya looked at me with a slight hesitation. Fortunately, her freak ass girlfriend Bella supported the nasty idea wholeheartedly; she said, "Yeah Maya, suck my pussy juice off his pretty dick."

I could feel Maya's hand take me out of Bella's pussy and into her mouth. The change of texture and temperature made my dick throb like crazy. Bella patiently waited for me to return to her pulsating pussy.

After a while, I told Maya, "Put my dick back in Bella." Bella enthusiastically agreed, "Yeah, put it back in me." Bella lifted up slowly and then lowered herself onto my dick deliberately.

After about five minutes, the women switched positions. Maya struggled to ride my pony while Bella devoured both of my balls into her mouth, twirling her tongue like a cheerleader's baton.

In a flash, images of Bella and Maya were side by side on their backs, at the bed's edge; me dipping my dick back and forth between their pussies. It was pure perfection. Secretly I wanted to stick my dick and Bella's ass, but I didn't even try. I needed something to look forward to the next time I was with them.

What I couldn't resist was turning out Maya. Bella was a super-freak, so having her take the lead into the nastier stuff was a no-brainer. While fucking Maya, I signaled Bella, "Psst, come over here and lick Maya's pussy while I fuck her. Bella hopped up and perfectly positioned her face downward, her cheek atop Maya's pubic hair, her tongue dancing on Maya's clit.

Bella's mouth was in the perfect position for me to slide my dick directly in after pulling out of Maya's warm wet box, so I did that shit—repeatedly. I took my dick directly from Maya's pussy to Bella's drooling mouth more often than I needed. My actions weren't just for my own pleasure.

My repetition was a way of teaching Maya the process. She liked calling me Daddy, and I was there to teach. I instructed her to look. "Look how good Bella eats your pussy and sucks my dick." After several additional rounds of back-and-forth, I asked Maya, "Do you think you could be a good bitch like Bella?"

Bella giggled. "I'm the bad bitch here." I reveled in the competition for my attention and pleasure. I instigated, "Come on, Maya, you gonna let her show you up like that?" The hesitation that was in Maya's eyes had disappeared, replaced with the determination to compete, a competition to see who would be my freakiest bitch, and I loved every filthy moment.

Within a few seconds, the girls had switched positions, and it was Maya's turn to watch me fuck Bella and clean her pussy juices off of my dick with her wet warm mouth. Initially, she was hesitant and clumsy. "Come on, Maya, you can do better than that, babe," I said, hoping to encourage her.

It worked, with a few more rounds of back-and-forth; Maya knew just when to grab my dick when Bella lifted her pussy during her riding routine.

Maya made the most of her turn, hungrily bobbing her head up and down on my dick, occasionally choking, and consistently slurping Bella's pussy juices from my shaft, before putting my dick back in Bella's pussy.

Once I was back inside Bella, I could feel Maya flickering her tongue across the base of my dick. I looked down just in time to see Maya spit directly onto Bella's pussy, keeping things juicy.

A few minutes later, I heard the words I had wanted to hear all night. Bella looked back at me and said, "Put your dick in my ass, Papi." I felt my dick surge. My anal fetish was about to be fulfilled. "You damn right," I said.

I removed my dick from her pussy and slid it slowly into her ass. Still, in a riding position, Bella slowly slid down my shaft, moaning louder the more her asshole opened, taking in more of my dick.

Maya knew the drill; she sucked on my balls, and I was in heaven. A tight asshole on my dick and a warm wet mouth devouring my balls, just how I should always be treated.

I turned Bella over, face down and her ass up. Her light brown booty hole winked at me, so I plugged it with my hard dick. First, she moaned, and a few seconds later she screamed as I worked ten of my eleven inches in and out of her asshole.

I glanced over at Maya, who was watching at that point. She was next to get her ass fucked, and she knew it. I could tell by the nervous look in her eyes. Seeing her waiting patiently for anal punishment increased my sexual experience to a drug high.

When I tried to get my dick in Maya, I could tell she was new at taking dick up her ass. Perhaps an anal virgin, my favorite. Bella started off tight and then opened for me, but Maya's asshole had a death grip on my dick from the first inch up to the ninth.

Just about ten inches was all I could get inside her before she screamed at the top of her lungs. "Oh my God, my ass is on fire." I told her, "No, that's just my fire hose bitch."

Bella gave Maya gentle kisses on her face while I fucked her ass good. Maya seemed to get into the experience, screaming my name. "Santé!... Oh my fucking God. Santé!" I had to give the bitch points for honesty. With almost ten inches of Puerto Rican dick in her ass and with me stroking towards the full eleven inches of heaven, I was her God. And from the smirk on my face, I'm sure it was obvious to both of my bitches, I knew it.

I wanted to work Maya's ass open a bit more, but her asshole was still tight even after ten minutes of slamming it. Maya's ass felt so good and so tight I couldn't keep fucking her like I wanted. I was going to cum if I didn't pull out fast.

Because I didn't want my freak bitches to miss a drop of daddy's juice, I told both of them to lie flat on their backs. I straddled both girls, pushing them as close as possible. "Both of you squeeze your tits together." I said.

I could tell from Bella's expression and her touching her tits, she assumed I was gonna cum on their titties. I actually just wanted them closer between my legs so I could rain cum down onto their faces.

My balls tightened. "Lick your lips, no even better, kiss each other," I demanded with urgency and domination.

My obedient bitches followed instructions. Bella, the belle of the ball, once again exceeded my expectations by flickering her tongue and licking around the outline of Maya's lips.

The site caused me to explode; I was cumming. Heaps of white juice leaped from my dick. The first wad made a "Splat" sound on Bella's cheek. Without needing to provide instruction, the Mexican hottie took her index finger, scooped my cum with it, and fed Maya directly.

Then, my massive rainstorm occurred. Waves of pleasure and muscle contractions underneath my balls cause my body to jerk. Sweat suddenly poured from my forehead. Momentarily I felt lightheaded, lost in the warm haze; my eyes slowly lowered to see

Bella and Maya playfully swirling their tongues and swapping my cum back and forth in each other's mouths. Their lips were glazed like freshly dipped donuts.

My body grew limp. I touched the wall of the swimming pool, and I was spent. I inhaled deeply several times before lowering myself under the swimming pool's surface. There was no splashing; the water above stayed smooth, chill, and peaceful.

Pushing through the water from deep under the pool's center, I felt lighter again, making me float slowly to the top. The soft trickling of water falling from my head felt like I was being washed clean. I was refreshed; but so much more... Once again, I was reborn.

*She fell into his eyes like deep water—
by the time she surfaced, she was already on her knees.*

CHAPTER TWENTY-ONE

TRAMPOLINE DREAMS

When Jackie arrived with my kids at 6 AM, she looked at me like she deserved a trophy for bringing them back earlier than the two weeks she'd promised to keep them from me.

I didn't give her the reaction she wanted, so at the 9 P.M., pickup, she didn't even bother to get out of her blue Toyota Camry.

Watching my kids stroll down the path to Jackie's blue Toyota Camry, I felt that familiar ache hit my chest. They turned and waved, their faces lit with innocent smiles, completely unaware of the sharp scalpel ripping through my chest every time they left me.

I closed the door and leaned against it. The house went dead quiet. I'd just had a wonderful Sunday with my kids, but it wasn't enough. It would never be enough. Not like before, when we all lived together, when the laughter and chaos in this house were constants, not just quick flickers.

I loved the freedom of my new life, making choices without someone constantly bitching at me. But I missed the routine I'd fought to build.

Jackie never got that my sacrifices, my efforts to cut back running the streets and me keeping my side bitches out of her face, wasn't just for the family. That shit was for my own healing too.

I didn't want to live through another broken family. I would never have left Jackie for Victoria, Kay, or any of the others. My parents' divorce fucked me up, and my father's death shattered me to my soul. I wanted to rebuild myself and eventually piece together a family that would last. So, when Jackie gave me the ultimatum to marry her, I knew it was time to grow up and build a family.

I wanted one that looked good, the kind of shit you see on TV. You know, the suburban single house, 2.1 kids, white picket fence, and a trampoline in the backyard. The kind of image that would make both of our families proud of me. Jackie and I had all of that, right down to the trampoline, until she cheated on me. I couldn't even pretend there was any way to come back from that. I'd take death before dishonor. So now I'm trying the bachelor life and still being a good father.

So, that Sunday was just for my kids. Junior and I played Uno; his competitive fire made me laugh. Young boi wasn't ten yet but already stood just under my armpit, growing like a weed. He loved polo shirts, a chip off the old block, which both amused and touched me.

Jovie, my little daddy's girl, almost seven, loved her unicorns and rainbows; her bright personality always shone through. She giggled endlessly as she rode on my back, playing horse; she was the only person I'd do that for in the world.

When I proudly asked, "Who wants pizza? I'm ordering pepperoni!" Excited cries of "Me!" filled the air. Even Mark, my stepson, joined in, his tough-guy teenage act slipping to reveal the boy underneath.

SANTE'S SECRET

The 75-inch TV was mainly for me when we all lived together, but on that Sunday, it became the centerpiece of our movie night. The smell of popcorn and pizza filled the house, mingling with their laughter. These moments mattered, and I shoved the memories into my heart.

But underneath it all, a deep, excruciating pain was still there—one I never spoke of, not to anyone. I felt like a failure. I didn't keep my family together. I was supposed to do better, to be better.

No matter how hard I tried, the ghost of my father, Eduardo Sabatino, haunted me. I loved him, but I needed to be a better father to my kids than he was to me. His absence left me empty in a way I was determined to fill, but every goodbye to my kids felt like ripping open an old wound.

Missing my father was a pain I carried silently, secretly. But, it was never far from my mind, affecting everything I did. I dealt with the pain by fucking bitches and having fun while staying active in my kids' lives.

I found myself trying to relive my childhood through their eyes. I wanted to be the father Eduardo couldn't be, to be present in a way he never was.

As I walked through the now-quiet house, memories of the past 24 hours played in my head like a movie. The joy in Jr.'s eyes when he won a game, the sound of Jovie's laughter, the way Mark tried to hide his smile—they were flashes of small moments in time, but they meant everything to me.

I sat down on the couch, staring at the dark TV screen. I could almost hear the echoes of their voices still in the air, and I clung to them, knowing the leftovers had to keep me going until the next visit. The house felt empty, but my heart was full, even if only for a while.

I picked up my phone and scrolled through my pussy options; maybe a good dick sucker to shake off my sadness. There were some top picks, but I figured they would all be too much effort. I was physically and emotionally spent. It was clear to me that if I was gonna have my balls drained, I'd have to do it myself.

I dashed to the window, pulled the curtains, then made a running leap back onto my black leather couch. Hitting the remote, the giant screen that showed PG-rated TV and movies just an hour ago was now glowing with a big titty bitch, getting face fucked.

Soon, my Tommy Hilfigers were off, slung across the floor, next to my coffee table, and I was free-ballin'. I reached into my couch's storage compartment for the extra creamy lotion. My bitches could catch the next round. This nut... was on me— literally.

CHAPTER TWENTY-TWO

THE JENGA INCIDENT

The grind of the machines and the sounds of welding downstairs faded as I leaped the steps two at a time. I shoved through the swing doors to the second floor, heading straight for the reception desk.

Up here, it's always cooler, quieter—like a different world. Elaine was behind the desk, glasses low on her nose, focused on her screen.

"Elaine." I barked, nodding her way.

She looked up, her serious expression lightened as recognition washed over her. "Santé," she said, a warm smile breaking through.

Without hesitation, I asked, "Is Joel around?"

Her fingers paused over her keyboard, and she tilted her head slightly. "No, he's away at another conference. He'll be back tomorrow. Only Kay is here right now."

Pretending to be disappointed, I said, "Alright, I'll return tomorrow then." I made a show of turning to leave, but after a few steps, I paused. "Actually, I'll just take the back steps down to the shop," I added, hoping to mislead her.

Elaine nodded, her attention already back on her computer. "Okay, have a good day, Santé."

With Elaine distracted, I slid toward the back offices, moving like I owned the place. As I got closer to the shared office area, I spotted Kay. She looked up from her desk, the only one of the three occupied. Her eyes widened when she saw me. I guess Kay caught me scoping out the gray, drab surroundings filled with metal desks and empty chairs because she smirked and said, "We're all alone; everybody's at lunch."

A mischievous grin appeared on my face. "Good." I growled, "Your lunch is in Joel's office."

Kay paused, her fingers poised over her keyboard. "Just let me finish this last blog entry," she asked, but I wasn't having any of that bullshit.

I groped my dick, cocked my head, then repeated my words slowly, "I said, Your lunch. is. in. Joel's. office."

Finally, Kay got the hint and abandoned her blog entry; she got her ass up and joined me in a mad dash toward Joel's office. As soon as the door closed behind us, Kay's professional attitude vanished, and so did my blue drawls.

With my underwear thrown on the floor, Kay's lips met my dick. Her moans let me know she was loving every second of our freak show. After sucking my dick's head and receiving passionate kisses to my balls, I remembered we didn't have much time.

I pulled Kay from her knees, turned her around, and pushed her onto Joel's desk. Kay lifted her skirt, and I pulled her panties to the side. I slid my dick inside Kay's wet, hot snatch. Her pussy walls quivered with a familiar signature.

I had just hit Kay's pussy with my fifth stroke when she moaned loudly. "Shhh," I said, not wanting to draw attention. She covered her own mouth, but any attempt at quiet was gone when I pounded that pussy on my seventh stroke.

"Clack-clack-clack; Crash!" Kay covered her head to avoid getting hit. Joel's extensive Jenga tower lay in smithereens. There were pieces on the desk, behind Kay, and several pieces on the floor, but through it all my dick never missed a stroke.

The right thing might have been to stop to gather the pieces and put them back together or at least sweep them into a neat pile, but that never happened.

Kay struggled to keep her hand over her mouth as I fucked her even harder and faster, assuming we had less time before we'd be discovered. I was going to get my lunchtime nut; Jenga pieces be damned.

Kay removed her hand from her mouth, and her passion was unleashed. "Oh, fuck me, Santé". I put my back into fucking her faster and harder. Her pussy got wetter. Face down on the desk, Kay gripped some of Joel's papers, and I laughed to myself.

I loved the reactions bitches had to my dick. Besides the good sensations I felt, the females' reactions made sex worthwhile for me.

I put a lot of effort into my stroke that afternoon. It had been many months since we had that length of time in Joel's office, and I wanted her to remember me, my power, her place, and most importantly, my dick.

"I'm cummin..." My announcement happened so fast that it even surprised me. Kay quickly scrambled to get on her knees to catch my cum. "Uhh," I muttered before cumming.

I eyed Kay as she gobbled down every drop of my thick, white, creamy cum. Her mouth and tongue moved so fast that she looked like a hungry refugee. The look in her eyes was an exotic blend of panic and praise.

After I was sure there was not so much as a speck of my cum remaining on her face or tongue, I picked up my blue briefs and hopped into them.

"Lunch is over," I said, my smirk sharp as I moved toward the door, stealing one last look behind me. The Jenga blocks lay scattered—discarded—like everything else I was leaving behind.

CHAPTER TWENTY-THREE

JAGGED TRUTHS OF THE PAST

The red walls of my lounge appeared to glow, adorned with abstract paintings and evocative photographs of forested landscapes. The warmth of the Friday evening was intensified by the soft, dim lighting overhead and the flickering vanilla candle on the windowsill.

The room had a complicated scent—the vanilla candle, my gardenia perfume, Santé's captivating Versace cologne, and a distant, comforting aroma of a sweet treat baking.

As I sat on one of the black leather loveseats and Santé on the red leather couch, I allowed my eyes to take in the details of Santé's appearance that evening. The striking blue of his ball shorts contrasted with his black Nike flip-flops, which lay discarded by the side, exposing his bare feet nestled in my black shag carpet.

His amber eyes, usually sparkled with mischief as he regaled me with naughty tales, but on the Friday evening of May 21st, they held a shadow I hadn't seen before.

"I just don't believe they'll ever consider me for the shop supervisor's position. Word is they think I'm too young to be supervisor." Santé's voice sounded distressed. Eliciting a surprising empathetic impulse, which I was determined to hold in check.

"Too young? That's not fair," I responded, my red-painted fingers fiddling with the hem of my one-piece jumper. "Is that even legal?" I asked.

Santé looked at me, tiredness in his gaze. "It might not be. But they'll find other reasons, other 'strikes' against me. They expect bonding outside of work, but until recently, all my free time was with my family."

There was a pause. I sensed there was more he was holding back. "You mean with Jackie?"

As he nodded hesitantly, I sensed a weight behind his words. "Since the divorce, I've just been... resting and reminiscing," he confessed, his voice trailing off. Then, almost as an afterthought, he added, "You know, if it weren't for a dude named Jagger, I would never have known the whole truth of why my marriage ended."

My heart skipped a beat at the mention of that name—Jagger. I thought, It couldn't be a coincidence, could it? I struggled to maintain my composure, to keep Santé from suspecting anything, as his words echoed in my mind.

I watched as he looked down at the carpet, his gaze distant, lost in memories. Slowly, gently, I prodded, peeling back the layers of his story like removing a band-aid from an old wound.

"Oh, I'm confused," I said, trying to hide the tremor in my voice. "Was the guy Jagger having an affair with your wife?"

"No, it was much more complicated than that," he replied, his tone heavy with resignation. "My wife was having an affair, and my mistress, Victoria, found out about it. Somewhere along the line, she told her best friend, Patricia, who was going with this guy named Jagger."

The pieces of the puzzle began to fall into place, each revelation more shocking than the last.

"Oh, wow," I murmured, struggling to process it all. "But I don't understand how Jagger came to tell you about your marriage."

"Well, apparently Victoria had this scheme," Santé explained. "She wanted me to find out about my wife's messing around without actually telling me. So, she hired somebody to get proof and then sent it to me anonymously. She shared that plan with her best friend."

"Her best friend, Patricia," I said, the realization dawning on me.

"Yeah, that was her," Santé confirmed. "And Pat's dude, Jagger, heard all about it. But it seems he had his own drama, where an ex-lover had broken up his marriage before he met Pat, so he decided to look out for me. To tell me the truth because he knew what it felt like to have a marriage get fucked up due to a jealous side piece."

"Wow," I whispered, the weight of Santé's revelation settling in my mind like stones slowly sinking in water.

"Yep, Jagger showed up at my job one day, clear out of the blue," Santé continued.

"And you believed him?" I asked, unable to contain my curiosity.

"Not at first," Santé admitted. "But he knew too much to be guessing. Sometimes you can just tell when people are telling you the truth... and at the same time, you realize someone close to you has been lying."

A moment of silence formed, but the burning sensation in my belly wouldn't allow me to change the subject.

"Did you say the guy's name was Jagger?" I asked, cautious but perhaps too eager.

"Yeah, what'ch-ya know him or something?" Santé replied, his brow furrowing in confusion.

"No, it's just... that Jagger is somewhat of a unique name," I stammered, struggling to maintain my composure.

"Well, he turned out to be a pretty unique dude," Santé remarked, a hint of admiration in his voice. "I kept his secret. Until now, I had never told anybody that he gave me the information. In fact, the last time I saw him was in the courtroom just before they sent Victoria to prison."

"Prison? Victoria went to prison?" I echoed, my voice filled with feigned ignorance and false surprise.

Santé must've realized he had spoken too much. "That's enough about Victoria, Jagger, and that whole messy past," he said abruptly, changing the subject. "Let me think of some juicier stories I think you'd rather hear."

The atmosphere grew thick with a shared, anxious silence. Pushing aside my secret knowledge, I ventured, "Last question—was the divorce your idea or hers?"

His eyes met mine. "It was mutual." The silence returned, but it felt heavier this time. His gaze fell on the black shag rug beneath our feet.

We sat in silence, the hum of the dimly set recessed lighting filling the space.

A light beep sounded. Santé looked puzzled, and fear struck my heart. Just then, as if on cue, the timer from my kitchen buzzed, breaking the tense stillness. I rose. "Excuse me for a moment." I excused myself just in time.

Walking on the tiled floor of my yellow and white kitchen, I opened the oven; the rich aroma of red velvet cupcakes wafted into my nostrils. I carefully placed four of them on a platter and headed back to my lounge.

Returning, I found Santé in a light slumber on the couch, the lines of stress smoothed out, giving him a peaceful and innocent appearance. As I gently placed the platter of cupcakes on the coffee table, the slight clink of ceramic on the glass table stirred him awake.

"I'm so sorry, Santé," I whispered, feeling guilty.

He smiled slightly. "I was just resting my eyes. It's been a long week. I've been working hard," he said.

His fleeting vulnerability touched me. "Any plans for the weekend?" I asked.

"Not really," he admitted.

"Well," I began, struck with an idea, "Maybe you could invite your coworkers and boss for a cookout. Might help with that promotion."

The sea foam green within his eyes shone vividly. "That's brilliant! I should start planning right away." He said, raising quickly, his excitement palpable.

"But the cupcakes," I protested with a grin.

"I'll take two to go," he added, "and save some for when I come back." He winked.

I laughed, and as he approached me, he placed a soft kiss on my cheek, his Versace cologne lingering. Without another word and without needing direction, he strode confidently to my front door, calling out, "Manda, I'm locking the bottom lock!"

"Okay," I replied; the door's soft click echoed the changing dynamics between us. But what did it mean for my mission? I couldn't help but feel a mixture of excitement and apprehension. Nevertheless, I knew two things for certain: first, things were getting very complicated, and second, I had to speak to Isaac—about Jagger.

CHAPTER TWENTY-FOUR

SANTÉ'S WEB

The evening settled into an air of tension, like the calm before a storm. I sat in my lounge, the red walls glowing softly around me, cradling a mug of cinnamon tea, savoring its warm, spicy scent. I held the phone to my ear, waiting for Isaac to pick up.

"Hey, Mandy, what's up?" Isaac's voice was easy, unaware of the storm about to break.

"Isaac, there's something I need to ask you," I started, the words tumbling awkwardly. "But, um, it's a bit complicated."

"Okay..." Isaac trailed off, his tone shifting as he sensed my hesitance. "Sound off, girl. What's going on? Is this about Santé?"

I hesitated, my heart pounding. "It's... sort of about Santé, but it's more about you, actually."

"About me?" His confusion was palpable, a sharp note of surprise cutting through the line.

"Well, it could be about you," I said, hedging.

Isaac was silent for a moment, then his voice sharpened with urgency. "Mandy, you need to give it to me straight. What's going on?"

I took a deep breath, the air heavy in my lungs. "I know I said I wouldn't bring up Jay anymore, but... I have to ask you something."

"Sure," Isaac replied, a tremor of trepidation in his voice.

"What's J's real name?" I asked directly, bracing for his reaction.

Isaac paused, a silence stretching between us. "Why are you asking about that? You know 'J' was a codename for Jagger."

I closed my eyes momentarily, gathering the courage for what came next. "Isaac, don't get too alarmed, but there's something unexpected I found out from Santé. It involves Jagger."

Isaac made an audible gasp, the sound sharp in my ear. "What? Amanda, what are you talking about?"

"Santé told me a story," I began, my voice dropping to a whisper as I leaned back against the plush couch cushions. "He mentioned Jagger in a way... I wasn't expecting."

"Go on," Isaac urged, his voice tense.

"Santé was opening up about his past, especially after his divorce. He said, if it weren't for someone named Jagger, he wouldn't have known the whole truth about why his marriage ended." My fingers tightened around the mug, the ceramic warm against my skin.

Isaac was silent, and I could almost hear his mind racing. "And what did Jagger do exactly?"

"It's twisted, Isaac," I continued, my voice thick with the unfolding drama. "Santé's wife was cheating on him, and his mistress, Victoria, found out. She decided to expose the affair but didn't want to be the one to tell Santé directly. So, she concocted a plan to have someone else send him the evidence anonymously."

"And Jagger was involved in this plan?" Isaac's tone was incredulous.

"Yes, but not like you think. Victoria told her best friend, Patricia, about the plan, and Patricia was dating Jagger. He learned about it and decided to step in.

He told Santé the truth himself, out of empathy, I guess. I think he really felt for Santé, you know? A few years back, Jagger's own world got turned upside down. He had his own affair. From what I gathered, when he tried to break it off, the woman went nuts. She told his wife everything to get back at him, which blew up his marriage. Totally messed him up.

Seeing Santé in a similar bind and with that whole bro code phenomenon, I guess he just couldn't stand by and watch it happen all over again. I guess he thought he was doing Santé a solid by telling him the truth before it was too late.

Isaac exhaled sharply. "This is a lot to take in. So my Jagger was trying to help Santé?"

"Exactly," I said. "Jagger even showed up at Santé's job one day, out of nowhere, to tell him everything. Santé was skeptical at first, but he said Jagger knew too much to be making it up."

There was a pause as Isaac digested the information. "I... I had no idea about any of this. Jagger never mentioned—"

"He kept it a secret," I interrupted, my voice low. "Until now, Santé never told anyone else that Jagger was the one who came forward. It's a mess, Isaac, a real mess."

Isaac's breathing was heavy; a distant rustle of movement suggested he was pacing. "And you're telling me this because..."

"Because I thought you needed to know the truth. The full scope of it," I finished, the last words hanging between us like a delicate thread about to snap.

"Thank you, Mandy," Isaac said finally. Isaac let out a long whistle. "Wow, Mandy, you just dropped a whole season finale on me in one call! But listen, this whole mess just confirms my gut feeling about Santé. I knew he reminded me of Jagger, and now it turns out they are both cut from the same cloth." He added, "You've got to tread carefully around him, okay? You're peeling back layers of a man wrapped up in all this drama. It's like navigating a minefield."

I could hear the concern laced through his sassy tone, and I knew he was right. "I know, Isaac. It's a lot to take in. I'll be careful, I promise. After all, it's all for the book, right?"

Isaac's voice softened, the sass giving way to sincerity. "And hey, thanks for filling me in. Seriously. It actually clears up a lot about that night Jagger showed up at my apartment. I always wondered what led him to my door that night, and the sex that followed. It's like getting the last piece of a puzzle—except this one's more twisted than any jigsaw I could have ever imagined."

I chuckled despite the gravity of our conversation. "Only the best puzzles for us, right?"

"Exactly, girl!" Isaac exclaimed. "But really, Mandy, this explains so much. It's messed up, but it also helps me see my time with Jagger in a new light. I guess sometimes you really don't know what's going on behind the scenes."

"Yeah, it's sad, really." I sighed, looking out at the darkening sky through the window. "Everyone's just trying to find their way through their own mess."

"True that," Isaac agreed. "But you, my dear, make sure you stay out of the whirlpool of drama. Take notes, but don't get a starring role in their play of messiness. Leave the soap opera and stunts to Santé and his crew."

I smiled, warmth spreading at Isaac's typical blend of humor and heartfelt advice. "I will. And thanks, Isaac. It feels better talking this out with you."

"Anytime, girl," he said. "You know I'm here for the gossip and the deep talks, whatever you need."

We said our goodbyes, and I felt mixed emotions as I hung up the phone. There was relief in sharing the burden of the secret, worry for the entangled lives I was studying for my book, and gratitude for having Isaac to help navigate the complexities of friendships and love.

As the last echoes of our conversation lingered, I realized that understanding the past could change the present and perhaps even shape the future.

But for now, I needed to keep my eyes open and my heart guarded. Isaac was right; in this tangled web of truths and lies, caution was my best ally.

CHAPTER TWENTY-FIVE

CHARCOAL AND CHARADES

The smell of hotdogs and hamburgers wafted through the air, mingling with the scent of grass. The vibrant colors of the clear blue sky and the high green grass made Santé's backyard feel surreal.

I glanced around the yard, taking in the sight of Santé's friends and co-workers chatting animatedly, their voices blending into the background music playing at a low volume coming from the two tall gray speakers.

A man that I would come to know as Fred, approached me with a grin, his eyes sparkling. His Hawaiian shirt, loud and colorful, added to his playful demeanor. He took a case of beer and said, "Don't you look absolutely stunning?" His tone was flirtatious. "I don't think we've met. I'm Fred, Santé's friend and part-time fan."

As Fred extended his hand, I tried to absorb the oddity of his statement. Fred added, "I'm also his coworker." I smiled, shaking his hand. "Nice to meet you, Fred. I'm Amanda, Santé's new next-door neighbor."

Fred's grin widened. "You picked a great day to come over. Santé is throwing one of his rare cookouts, the first since... Well, come on over." He ended his sentence never completing his thought.

We moved closer to the crowd, the murmurs of conversations becoming clearer. Fred's voice rose above the others, "I didn't know Santé had such a good looking, sexy neighbor." Fred's tone remained awkwardly flirtatious. "You know, Santé is single now." I glanced towards Santé.

Fred spoke loudly. "Hey Santé, any chance you'd be open to dating your beautiful new neighbor?" I noticed Santé, who was nearby, caught Fred's comment. Santé's eyes darted to me, a flicker of surprise passing through them.

Before Santé or I could respond, a woman in a blue maxi dress nearby started coughing violently. Standing next to her, a man that I would come to know as Joel quickly fetched a glass of lemonade, his concern evident in how he handed it to her, his brow furrowed.

"Here you go, Kay," Joel said, his voice soothing. "Take a sip and breathe."

Kay nodded, gratefully taking the lemonade and sipping it slowly.

As her coughing subsided, I took a step closer to her. "Hi, I'm Amanda," I said softly, not wanting to distress her. "I just moved in next door."

Kay managed a weak smile between sips. "Hey, I'm Kay."

"Sorry about that," Santé said to me, his voice milder than I had become used to as he turned towards me. "Fred can be a bit much sometimes."

Joel shook his head, a slight smile on his lips. "No offense, Amanda, but Fred is off on this one. I still think Santé and Jackie will get back together."

Santé's reaction was subtle but noticeable. His eyes widened slightly, and he glanced away, his jaw tightening. He fiddled with the tongs in his hand, the metal clinking softly. "Not every married couple has a fairytale ending like yours, Joel," Santé replied, his voice sounding strained but calm. Santé looked at Kay and then in my general direction when he said, "But who knows, maybe one day I'll be open to dating again."

I could feel the tension in the air, the awkwardness settling like a heavy fog. The conversation shifted to lighter topics, and I found myself drawn to the trampoline in the corner of the yard. It was a visual reminder of Santé's former family life, symbolizing the past he was still grappling with.

With a beer in hand, it was apparent Joel was Santé's boss. He chipped in, "I have a talented team. And I'm not just talking about my welders. Kay here is a budding blogger and quite the sensation!"

Kay, slightly shifting her stance, appeared to blush as she responded, "Come on Joel, It's just a small side gig."

I tilted my head curiously. "Oh? So, you're a writer?"

For the only time that afternoon, Kay appeared unguarded as she said, "I hope to be one, someday."

Joel chuckled, "Small blog maybe, but already influential and a trusted source of information. It's my daily morning read."

A hint of pride glimmered in Kay's eyes. "Thanks, Joel."

Amidst the chuckles, Fred reached for a new beer, then declared, "If my wife calls, I've had just this one beer, okay?"

Laughter erupted, but Santé's face showed evident disapproval as he strolled to the grill.

Planted where he stood, Joel added, "No more beer for me today. I want my words to match my actions. Lying, especially to one's wife, isn't wise."

Santé smirked, turning from the grill with a plate in hand, "That's our resident Saint, no lying." Santé added, "Unless it's about buying another Jenga set." Santé's voice dripped with sarcasm.

Laughter rang out again; Joel appeared emotionally chafed but feigned amusement and good cheer, saying, "There are exceptions."

I raised an eyebrow, "Jenga?"

Fred leaned in, "It's Joel's guilty pleasure."

As the laughter ebbed, the conversation turned to work. I was introduced to Santé's other coworkers: Brian, José, Paul, and Lee.

José initiated shoptalk, "Those shipping containers need finishing by Tuesday."

Rolling his eyes, Paul asked, "And whose idea was it to accept such a tight deadline?"

José didn't back down. "I said it because I think it can be done."

Brian sat beside Lee, and interjected, "If we utilize the MIG welding technique, we might manage. It's faster for thicker materials."

Lee, scratching his head, said, "MIG's good but we should ensure we're not compromising strength. The weight they'll bear is enormous."

Santé, seizing the moment to display his prowess, interrupted as he strutted over, "TIG welding is what we should use. It's neater."

Lee frowned, "TIG's great for precision, but it's slower and not ideal for this scale. MIG is our best bet."

Joel may have sensed the shift in mood and diplomatically intervened. "Technically, Lee's right about MIG being more suitable for this. But Santé, I get the quality you're aiming for."

There was an awkward pause, and then, seemingly oblivious to the tension, Lee asked, "Santé, when you get a chance may I have some chocolate milk?"

Brian and José chuckled quietly. Given the environment, Lee's request seemed odd. From my vantage point, I could see a flicker of annoyance across Santé's face, but he quickly composed himself.

"Lee, this is a cookout, but if you want chocolate milk, I'm the kind of host and 'team player' who will get you chocolate milk."

I watched as Santé cut a look toward Joel, as he said 'team player,' a fleeting glance that spoke volumes.

It was clear Santé wanted to impress his boss and show that he was a team player willing to go the extra mile. I could see the effort he was putting into maintaining his composure, the way he carried himself with a mix of dignity and restraint. I pondered, was Santé evolving?

As the conversation flowed back to welding and workplace antics, I found myself observing Santé more closely. The sounds of laughter and chatter filled the air, but my attention remained fixed on Santé.

While the gentle breeze rustled the leaves of the nearby trees, adding a soft, natural melody to the afternoon, Fred's earlier comment suddenly echoed in my mind. I couldn't help but wonder what it would be like to date someone like Santé.

I could practically hear Isaac's voice in my head; come on bitch, get a hold of yourself. This is a mission, not a marriage. I found it psychologically fascinating that I could understand the danger of his pattern of behavior yet feel a slight attraction.

As the day wore on, I realized that this cookout was more than just a social gathering—it was a window into Santé's world, a glimpse into the complexities that defined him. And in that moment, I felt a connection, a spark of understanding that left me both intrigued and eager to learn more.

Yet, I decided it was time to leave. The intense emotions and the palpable tension were overwhelming, and I needed a moment to collect my thoughts. I stood up, brushed the grass from my clothes, and made my way towards my own property.

"Thanks for the cookout, Santé," I said, giving him a small wave. He looked up, surprised, and nodded.

"Anytime, Amanda. Take care," he replied. All of Santé's co-workers said goodbye to me with the notable exception of Kay. She stayed silent, her gaze fixed elsewhere as if I didn't exist. With one last glance at the scene behind me, I walked around the side of Santé's house, stepping closer to my home.

The sounds of laughter and conversation faded into the background. The afternoon sun cast long shadows on the front lawn as I crossed onto my property line. My mind buzzed with the day's events and the enigmatic presence of Santé Sabatino.

CHAPTER TWENTY-SIX

MILK, MISCHIEF, AND MOVES

As I entered the kitchen, Kay was already there, her hand frozen on the handle of my steel refrigerator door, her eyebrows arched as if surprised to see me in my own house.

"You know," she began, her tone playful, "I thought you'd abandoned me." Kay paused dramatically, with a smile on her lips. Like so many times before.

I could feel the echoes of our past as I gripped a small metal box from my cabinet, pushing her words aside. "I told you I'd be in touch, and here we are."

"You know...in over ten years, this is the first time I've been in your house," she remarked, walking the length of the kitchen. Her heels clicked on my sandalwood-colored flooring.

The low hum of the dishwasher, mixed with the smell of barbecue and beer, set the scene for our tense exchange. It was almost funny, the way the tension crackled between us while the cookout a few feet away was all laughs and good times.

Kay's eyes darted to the slender window, catching sight of our coworkers outside, laughing and kicking it, with "Kiss Me More" by Doja Cat playing low in the background. She smirked. "Not a bad cookout you threw together, considering it was a last-minute affair."

I could tell Kay was being bitchy, her choice of the word 'affair'. I thought I'd dick-slap her later. I also considered explaining the role of a mistress. Instead, I placed the box down on the gray countertop. "Jackie never wanted guests," I replied, blaming my ex-wife for the secrecy.

I wasn't about to dive deeper into our decade-long secret creeping. My focus was on Lee. I was already pissed from his earlier comments, acting like I didn't know my way around welding. But his annoying ass didn't stop there. I said, "Everyone's drinking beer, and Lee asks for chocolate milk. Did you hear that shit?"

Kay remarked, "Yeah, I caught that; what does he think he's in third grade?"

Keeping my rage under control, I headed to the pantry. Snatched a can of chocolate powder, then hit the fridge for a half-gallon of whole milk. As I set the milk down, my eyes landed on the special metal box on the counter, and I couldn't help but smirk.

"What are you up to?" Kay asked with a sly glint in her eyes.

I tossed some chocolate powder into a glass and splashed in a bit of milk. Popped open that special box, used the same spoon to scoop out the mysterious white stuff, and dumped it right in. I stirred it up real good, then topped off the glass with more milk.

Kay's eyes widened as a realization dawned on her. "Laxative?"

"Lee likes to talk a lot of shit. It's the perfect recipe," I replied smugly.

A nervous giggle escaped her. "You're really doing this?"

"Yes, we are," I teased, handing her the spiked drink.

She paused, then questioned, "We?"; the reality of what I was asking of her—instantly clear. I tilted my head just enough so the sunlight from the window hit my amber eyes, bringing out those hues of green and red. I knew I had her; it was a move I knew affected all of my bitches.

As I suspected, her resistance melted like an ice cube on a hot grill. She exhaled and slowly said. "Alright."

Our little scheme made the bond between us even tighter. The hum of the dishwasher, the sizzle of meat on the grill, the low chatter from the backyard—all of it faded into the background. Right then, it was all about us and that spiked drink.

I felt a wave of satisfaction watching Kay strut toward the backyard, glass in hand. My plan was in motion, and I had one of my most loyal bitches to thank for it.

Kay handed Lee the concoction and completed the mission.

When she strolled back in, Kay said, "The things I do for you."

I ignored her comment and locked eyes with her when I asked, "You still got that key to Joel's office?"

Kay raised an eyebrow, looking a bit puzzled. "Yeah, it's in my desk at work. Why?"

"I'll give you the details later. I just need to know that you have my back," I leaned in and whispered, "And my front too," my voice thick with double meaning.

As the mellow beats played outside, I said, "Since it's your first time in my spot, I think I owe you a tour." Kay smiled and nodded. "That sounds nice."

I glanced out the window. Joel was out there, pulling meat off the grill. The sight almost had me heated again, but then I remembered I had given him permission before the whole Lee's welding comment.

I glanced at Kay's dick-sucking lips, which brought me back to the moment, and said, "I think my guests can take care of themselves for a while."

As before, I found my golden ray of light shining through the window. I made sure my eyes would sparkle, groped my dick, and said, "I think we should start your tour of my crib with the basement." The hint of kink in my voice was unmistakable.

*She fell into his eyes like deep water—
by the time she surfaced, she was already on her knees.*

CHAPTER TWENTY-SEVEN

BASEMENT BOTTOM

Man, basements have a vibe about them. Dark, a lil' mysterious, a touch on the forbidden side. So, mixin' that with my hard dick on Kay's tongue—and you're talking about a good time.

We were down there, right below the noses of my coworkers, when Kay began suckin' the fuck outta my dick; it was exhilarating. I had already got bold, pullin' off my tank top coming down the stairs. The cooler air of the basement teased my skin, but the heat from Kay's warm hand cupping my balls kept me just right.

When I kicked my shorts off a few seconds later, I was naked, barefoot, and horny as hell, getting basement head. Kay's sky blue maxi dress was perfect for the freaky occasion.

An old school jam 'oochie wally' echoed from the yard upstairs. Its beat seemed to sync with Kay's bobbing head. I stared at her big, pretty lips as she drew back from the base, towards the head of my meat. Her head jerked to the rhythm, her curves outlined by the faint light.

Feeling the moment, I took the initiative, slidin' closer, givin' her more of my Puerto Rican pepperoni. She whispered, her voice all raspy and shit, "You always know just how to feed me this dick, Daddy."

I smirked. "You damn right, bitch." My voice rumbling, my gaze locking onto her deep brown eyes. They had this mischievous glint, daring me to pump her mouth faster. And man, did I take that dare.

Sounds of dick slurping echoed off the bare concrete walls. The smell of grilled burgers and hot dogs drifted from above, mixing with the cool, earthy scent of the unfinished basement. My senses were all tangled up: the music, the smell, and the warmth of Kay's mouth deep-throating my dick. It was the perfect kind of get-together.

I ran one of my hands through my hair and gripped Kay's hair with the other. A low, sultry moan from Kay's voice box sent shivers up and down the shaft of my dick and vibrated in my balls.

Kay escaped my clutch long enough to breathlessly ask, "You think we're safe down here? What if someone comes lookin?"

I chuckled, "Down here, it's just you and me, girl. No one else matters." I walked over to the wall on the opposite side of the basement and leaned back. Kay quickly followed, drool dripping from her lips. The cool concrete against my back hit different against Kay's warm hands, one on my leg and the other rolling my balls between her fingers.

I watched as her dark eyes scanned me, adoring me, making me hyper-aware of her every move, every breath across my nuts. While on her knees, she took both of my balls in her mouth. Kay stroked my dick with one hand and reached upward with the other. Her fingers gently traced patterns on my chest, her touch light as a feather but burning every nerve it touched.

With my dick back in her mouth, I pumped her face to the upbeat tempo of the next song; our sex was like a dance. Her large, milky white titties bounced in rhythm, while her pink bra struggled to keep her ripe melons leashed. The realization that just a floor above, my coworkers were none the wiser made the moment even more delicious.

Kay pulled my dick out of her mouth and held most of it in her hand; the remaining inches dangled in the air; I could feel the warmth of her breath teasing my dickhead. A few seconds later she allowed my full eleven inches to dangle freely in the damp basement air. Her hands slowly slid down my legs, leaving trails of fire along the way.

Maybe it was the cookout above, or the secrecy of our lil' freaky get-a-way, but something made me wanna take it up a notch. "Stand up and bend over," I said with bass. Kay's eyes widened as she glanced up at me, clearly taken aback. But like a good bitch, she followed my directions.

Once bent over, I lifted her maxi dress. Kay's voice quivered with nervousness. "You sure about this?" she whispered.

As I mounted her, I murmured, "I've never been surer about anything in this world... I'm'a fuck you up your ass."

Kay let out a loud gasp, and her body tremored. I grabbed my dick and pushed it up against her tight hole. I grinned, wrapping my hands around her shoulders. I pulled her back onto my dick, feelin' the intensity she cried out, "Oh my God!"

I said, "There you go; that's what you've been needing, ain't it, bitch?" My voice was low, dripping with domination and anticipation.

Kay squealed, "Yes, Daddy, I've been a bad bitch. I need a good ass-fuckin.'"

Kay wasn't wearing any panties, so nothing was blocking my target. After years of fucking Kay's asshole, she opened up for me like I had an encrypted passcode. Kay was a grown-ass woman but still had plenty of grip. That said, her asshole and insides still formed around my dick like a perfect mold.

The party was in full swing upstairs; the muffled beats of hip-hop thumped from the ceiling, while I danced in Kay's asshole in the basement. Our forbidden dance of dick to ass was in full effect, but away from prying eyes.

One of Kay's tits finally escaped her bra, and I quickly cupped it. My fingers groped for her hard, pencil eraser-sized nipples. My large hands squeezed and rubbed them, making her asshole flex and flutter.

Our bodies moved in sync with the distant beats, but were dancing to our own sexy song. The temperature seemed to rise a few degrees. I could feel beads of sweat forming.

Kay's moans became louder as I picked up the pace, fucking faster than even the fastest beat. Before long I was slamming her asshole hard, like an angry child's tantrum on a toy. The sound of the impact was like thunderclaps on a silent night.

There was something about the pull of Kay's asshole muscles on my dick that always made me cum strong. I could feel the sensation building. I didn't want to cum inside of her; I wanted her to swallow. So I pumped faster, then faster still.

Kay's yelps became so loud I had to cover her mouth. Her muffled screams only brought me closer to the edge of cumming. I was really close, and I knew it. Finally, I gave her asshole one final hard dick slamming, which sounded like a gavel declaring a judgment.

My words tumbled out of my mouth rapidly and with a no-nonsense tone. "Turn around and open your mouth." Kay scrambled to follow my directions. She knew the deal. She positioned herself perfectly under my balls, her mouth gaping like a baby bird with an open beak; her mouth ready for nourishment.

"Ahh!" I thundered, my knees slightly buckling. My dick towered over Kay's face below, gushing powerful spurts of cum. Like my basketball game, my aim was impeccable; all six heaps of jizz landed in her mouth—swish.

Apart from Victoria, Kay was my most skilled bitch, so I trusted her to know what came next. Sure enough, Kay pushed my cum up for my inspection and waited. "Go ahead, swallow." I granted permission.

Kay swallowed all of my cum, but slowly.

Man, Kay's face was all lit like she was savoring the finest wine. She relished every drop of my jizz like it was the best thing she'd ever tasted.

Then, with no direction, she licked at the long sticky droplets of cum that streamed from my dick's head.

At last, my balls were officially empty—I was at peace. Moments like that were what I lived for.

But like the beauty of a sunset, once it was over, it was over. I pushed back and walked away, my dick swinging in silence. I was done, so I picked up my ball shorts and strolled to my basement powder room.

Kay must have had a trace of my cum on her lips. As I turned on the water to the low-hanging sink, I glanced at my bitch in the vanity mirror. I caught her scooping up the last speck of my liquid gift, relishing the flavor as she licked her finger clean.

Soon, that cum was gone too. Washing my dick in the sink, a smirk formed as I peeped how much Kay appreciated every last drop of my milky delight. All in all, it was a satisfactory cookout—Santé style.

CHAPTER TWENTY-EIGHT

SMOKE AND MIRRORS

The loud chime of the doorbell startled me. I had been deep into transcribing Santé's voice from a handheld recorder, his narcissistic sex stories weaving a complex maze of deceit and charm.

I quickly hit the 'off' button and wedged the device between the red leather cushions of the couch in my lounge. Picking up my laptop, I raced to the door, the screen's soft glow casting eerie shadows along my path.

Approaching my front door, I saw a familiar silhouette dancing in the window's frosted glass. My breath caught a little; it was Santé.

"Just a sec!" I called out, my voice breathless.

The momentary delay gave me time to stash my laptop in the office nook, which, with its purple walls, was a brief sanctuary of calm. Spinning my black leather office chair around, I opened my desk drawer and slid the laptop inside. After taking a moment to collect myself, I dashed back to the door. Composure regained, I ran my fingers quickly through my tousled hair and plastered on what I hoped was a casual smile.

"Cookout's over already?" I quipped as I opened the door.

I was met with those unmistakable eyes. I had seen them at least fifty times over the short period of knowing Santé Sabatino. Still, each time revealed something different, some new nuance.

This time, the yellow amber held a depth I hadn't noticed before. The red hues, usually so vibrant, appeared more subtle, almost pinkish, and the striking sea foam green, which usually captured my attention, was barely notable.

A shiver ran down my spine, but it wasn't cold. Santé gave a half-smile, his gaze never quite meeting mine. "It wrapped up twenty minutes ago," he replied, a touch of surprise in his voice as he continued. "But I'm amazed it lasted the four hours."

Tilting my head towards the kitchen, I offered, "Care for some cake? I might have a slice or two left."

Santé's laugh was airy. "I've just had dessert. Couldn't possibly stuff in anymore."

Something was off. "Want to talk in the lounge?" I ventured, hoping to bridge the sudden gap.

He chuckled, the sound hollow. "Yeah, I know the way." Following Santé, we settled into my lounge, the space between us on the couch speaking volumes.

"Did you catch Kay's icy stare today?" I asked, eager to break the silence.

His reply came slow and measured. "She's had feelings for me. But there's a line there... because of work."

I raised an eyebrow, recalling the many wild tales he'd shared. Had he forgotten all the sexual antics he shared with the workplace as the backdrop? "Coworkers? Seems unlike you to let that stop you."

He leaned forward, his eyes narrowing slightly. "There are still lines I don't cross," he began, "especially now, with someone like you in my life."

I narrowed my eyes as well, my lips parting slightly. "What do you mean?" I asked.

Santé's fingers played with a five-dollar bill before placing it on my glass coffee table. "Another story, for another five," he proposed, a mischievous glint in his eyes.

Without thinking, I found myself saying, "Deal."

But he raised a finger, the twinkle of mischief more intense. "Ah, but this time, after my story, you share something in return."

I hesitated before asking, "What could I possibly share that matches your stories?"

Santé stared at me, his gaze fixed. "Just tell me... what you're looking for?"

My stomach suddenly cramped with pain. Was I in danger? Was he suspicious? Cautiously, I repeated his words, "Looking for?"

His gaze was intense, pinning me to the spot. "Just tell me what you're looking for in a man."

A flurry of emotions welled up, leaving me feeling vulnerable and exposed. "Excuse me for a sec," I mumbled, almost sprinting to my first-floor powder room at the end of the hall.

Staring at my reflection, the magnitude of Isaac's warning crashed down on me. My mind raced with questions. Am I in over my head? I leaned against the sink, gripping its cool edge. I asked the question again, this time aloud. "Was Isaac right? Am I in over my head?"

The air felt thick, and my heart raced as I struggled to regain my composure. Wiping a tear from my eye and getting my hyperventilation under control, I couldn't fully explain the extreme nature of my physical reactions.

But I did know Santé had been alone in my lounge for almost ten minutes, so he would soon grow suspicious of my extended absence. Whether I was completely ready or not, I had to return to him and face whatever was developing.

*She fell into his eyes like deep water—
by the time she surfaced, she was already on her knees.*

CHAPTER TWENTY-NINE

THE GAME WAS ON

My charisma and sex appeal were undeniable. Women almost always spilled their guts around me, usually just before dropping their panties. A talent I sharpened over the years.

Amanda was no exception; I aimed to mold myself into her ideal man, which would give me direct access to the pussy. But tonight, something suggested I needed more direct tactics.

I had just asked Amanda what she was looking for in a man. She was so freaked out she turned pale. Maybe she wasn't used to a dude being so direct with her, but I thought, *she had better get used to it.*

Before she could answer my penetrating question, she dashed to the john. She had been gone for about two or three minutes before I pulled off my tank top. The cool air kissed my skin, my light golden complexion on full display. Amanda's scented candles, lavender, and vanilla played with my senses, as light smoke danced in the air.

When I sank into the red leather couch, an unexpected beep pierced through the smoky haze of the room. I remembered hearing the same sound during one of my previous visits. Then I thought I saw something; curious, my fingers brushed against a hidden device: A digital voice recorder.

I pressed play. There it was, my voice detailing my smut stories meant for Amanda's ears only. Bitch! My jaw clenched; Amanda's little spy game sent adrenaline rushing through my veins.

My pulse kicked up, anger fuckin with my thoughts. I reset the recorder, slipping it back in place, all while wondering just how deep Amanda's deception ran.

She drifted back into the room, voice soft but with a hint of concern. "Everything alright?" she asked, her eyes locking onto mine. The bitch was probably looking for some kind of angle. Trying to figure out if she could outplay me.

I was up on my feet quickly, closing the space between us before she even saw it coming. "It's late," I said, keeping it cool, hiding the fire burning inside. "And that five bucks... think of it as a down payment," I said.

"You sure?" She frowned, traces of confusion flickering across her face.

"Absolutely. Though next time," I paused, letting each word drip with meaning, "We share secrets at 'my' house."

Her hesitation hung in the air for a few tense seconds, but she eventually nodded. "Alright." she whispered—a surrender.

By the time we hit her front door, the calm sky over suburban Turnersville, New Jersey, was putting on its evening show. Even with the fire of betrayal still burning low inside me, I couldn't deny the soothing effect of the puffy clouds and the glow of the sunset above.

Right outside Amanda's door, I pulled her close. The day's fading warmth mixed with the evening's chill, was just like the heat between us, clashing against the cold shift inside me.

My voice, low and steady, cut through the quiet. "I probably shouldn't be saying this so soon," I murmured against her lips, "but I think I might be falling for you."

I kissed Amanda's lips softly. Her shoulders relaxed, and her eyes closed slowly. Damn, I'm good. I thought: *Even I felt a little moist, and I'm not even a bitch.*

When Amanda's eyes opened, they locked onto mine, confusion and something deeper swirling in them. I shook my head gently. "No words needed—my place, next Saturday." Amanda was speechless; a slow nod was her only response.

As I pulled back from her door and the moment, the silence surrendered slightly, letting in the faint sound of leaves rustling in the breeze. I strolled away, confidence in my stride.

My thoughts were spiraling but I couldn't help but smirk. My new discovery of Amanda's deception left a lot of questions and possibilities hanging in the air.

Although I didn't have all the answers, two things were crystal clear to me. One, Amanda was dabbling in a game way over her head. And number two, was as certain as that soft pink and lavender sky above. I was more pumped for the challenge ahead. I tugged my dick—the game was on!

CHAPTER THIRTY

TWO PATHS, ONE NIGHT

I felt my heart racing as the door closed behind Santé. Barely a second later, I was on Skype, calling Isaac. The window sparked to life.

"Santé was here," I blurted out.

Before I could hear Isaac's voice, I saw his concerned expression. I pressed on. "He had... things to say," I said reluctantly.

Isaac's eyebrow arched in a mix of intrigue and caution. "Things like what?"

I took a deep breath, gathered my courage, and let it all out. "He asked about what I wanted in a man, even said he had feelings for me. Wants our next secret-sharing session to be at his place. And... believe it or not, his visit ended with a kiss." I braced myself for Isaac's response.

His eyes widened. "Honey, are you kidding me? You are getting way too close to that man's sex pistol."

"What?" I snapped. Even for Isaac, this was a bit over the top.

He rephrased his warning, but not his message. "Okay, I'm going to say this in a way 'you' will understand... Girl, you in danger."

I sighed, my frustration mounting. "Isaac, I'm just doing my job! And guess what? He's also been texting me, with lots of spicy tales. I have more than enough for half the book now."

"Texts? You didn't mention anything about text messages!" Isaac exclaimed. "Amanda, do you even realize who Santé is? He's not just some guy; he's a master manipulator!"

I took a breath, trying to steady my rising annoyance. "Isaac, let's not forget, I'm the one with the license here. I've been trained to understand human behavior, and believe me, people are more layered than the profiles we create for them. And on a lighter note, this so-called master manipulator? He's hosting cookouts and even agreed to serve chocolate milk at a gathering because someone didn't want beer. Think about that."

Isaac's face contorted in disbelief. "Chocolate milk really, therapist Amanda?"

I retorted, "Chocolate milk is not the point. I'm saying there's more to him than our project. But for the book, I'll stick to his secrets," I said, trying to sound calm.

Isaac's expression hardened. "You're getting too involved, Amanda. It's clouding your judgment. If you can't stay objective, then maybe this project isn't right for us."

I countered, "You think I'm not working? Check Google Docs. I've shared the first draft of the manuscript with you."

Isaac blinked, stammering, taken aback. "I... I haven't checked yet."

I could feel my smirk forming. "Maybe you should. Before making snap judgments."

He took a deep breath. "Look, I'm flying out to L.A. for an interview with a major studio. They're discussing a bunch of productions, including whether your book would make a good film. Remember, I get the movie rights."

"I remember," I replied, "and I'm fine with that."

He paused, deliberation evident in his eyes. "I'll read what you've provided before I return. By Saturday morning, I'll be done."

I nodded. "Okay, and?"

Isaac stared at me, his gaze intense. "Saturday night, we'll talk. We'll decide whether to move forward with the book and the potential movie deal, or to shut it all down. But mark my words: Saturday night, you're talking to me. You're NOT jeopardizing both of our futures by being at Santé's."

Isaac's ultimatum hung heavy between us.

Isaac nodded, his look stern. "Saturday night, you're talking to me; or this whole operation is over. Understand?"

After a pregnant pause, I finally replied, "Understood."

I ended the call with my hands trembling. I couldn't be in two places at the same time, both demanding next Saturday night.

An evening with Santé to complete the mission and perhaps more, or I could satisfy Isaac's ultimatum, which still echoed in my ears.

I shook my head. How had my life come down to these two choices? And which one would I make?

CHAPTER THIRTY-ONE

LENSES AND LIES

After grinding through another long Tuesday on the factory floor, the sun was flexing its last bit of golden hour, casting streaks of light across the suburban streets. I rolled my tan Suburban toward my garage, remote in hand, expecting the door to rise smoothly like clockwork, welcoming me back to my kingdom. Instead, what greeted me was a massive box, parked dead in my spot, like it had been dropped there to start shit with me.

Two thoughts raced through my head. First, it'd been ages since a delivery guy got cozy using my garage code—something back in my married days, a time that now seemed so far away. It also dug up memories of Victoria and the chaos she'd carted in during her decade's tour of duty in my life. My second thought? That camera company's promise of 'overnight delivery' was no bullshit.

"Damn." I gave the box a hard look, sizing it up like some punk trying to step to me. The thing was solid, no lightweight, meaning whatever was inside wasn't just some cheap trinkets. My excitement started bubbling up as I grappled with it, feeling like a kid tearing into a giant cereal box, itching to get at the prize inside.

I slapped the car alarm as I bolted past my Suburban, the truck's horn giving a quick, supportive toot while I wrestled that beast of a box upstairs. The house was quiet, just the way I'd come to like it.

Reaching the top of the stairs, I dropped the box like it was on fire. Staring down at that cardboard cube, I wiped the sweat off my brow and grinned. The day's stress started to fade at the thought of tearing into my new gear.

With a knife still in my room from last night's dinner, I cut through the tape like a TV surgeon. The flaps opened up, revealing my new toys, gleaming under the hallway light like treasure.

For a moment, the world was just me and my shiny new gadgets, with no annoying coworkers, shipping containers to weld, or deceptive bitches. Just pure, unfiltered tech joy.

A half-hour later, my bedroom had turned into a storm of torn cardboard and bubble wrap. Hidden cameras of all sizes were spread out across my bed, along with a remote, Wi-Fi antennas, a DVR, and an instruction manual thicker than a sandwich.

With a smirk, I realized I was way ahead of the game. It was only Tuesday, and since my date with Amanda was set for Saturday night, I had plenty of time to master the new gadgets.

Holding the thick instruction book, I tossed my work jacket over a nearby chair and settled onto my bed. As I flipped through the pages, the room felt cooler, the sound of the AC blending with my thoughts.

After the lessons from my past, I learned you can never truly trust a bitch. Whether that's Victoria, my ex-wife Jackie, or now, Amanda, no woman could ever win my trust.

That thought led me to an even darker one: Could Amanda be working with Jackie, my ex? I tried to remember any looks from next door between them during Jackie's weekend drop-offs of the kids. Nothing came to mind, but that didn't kill the nagging feeling. With Jackie's endless scheming, I started picturing secret meetings between her and Amanda, plotting to squeeze me for more alimony or some other twisted revenge.

A smirk grew on my face. I muttered, "Amanda wants to play games? I've always been the king of games. In fact, I wrote the rulebook, Bitch." The idea of recording our evening brought a rush of adrenaline.

Not only would I get her to reveal her hand on camera, but I also planned to fuck her in front of the cameras too. First, I'd get Amanda sucking my dick on video from lots of good angles.

There's something about the visual of a bitch on video, sucking dick that would guarantee me keeping her in her place. Call it reputation insurance, a lil' something to keep her in line. Right or wrong, nobody respects a bitch looking into a video camera with a dick in her mouth; trust me on that one.

Pushing my paranoid thoughts aside, one thing was clear: I'd find out what Amanda was up to and have the evidence to back it up. Whatever her game was, she'd be shamed into playing along with me in the end.

The icing on the cake—I'd have a fuck show I could enjoy whenever I wanted some spank material. Saturday was shaping up to be one hell of a show.

CHAPTER THIRTY-TWO

PLOTTING A POWER MOVE

As I hustled up those worn front steps, moving from the shop floor to the upper offices of Manning & Mercer Containers, the usual ruckus—clanging metal, buzzing welders—faded out like a busted speaker. Each step was like turning down the static of a radio until I swung through those big ol' swinging doors into another world.

Man, just the distance of a few steps and a pair of creaky doors was like stepping from a hurricane into a Zen garden. No matter how often I came into the upstairs office, I never got used to how very different it was from the chaos downstairs where the neon green shirts like me worked.

The long front desk ruled the space, and there sat Elaine, queen of the front office throne, fingers flying across the keyboard like she was playing a piano.

"Elaine." I announced, easing into my lean on the reception counter and throwing her one of my trademark smirks. "I'm headin' back to holler at Joel. I just need to chop it up with him about that promotion."

Her fingers froze mid-tap, her eyes doing a little dance before finding mine. She cleared her throat, scrambling a bit. "Oh, Santé, good to see you, hun. You got an appointment?"

I chuckled, scanning the room. "Nah, no appointment, but figured Joel would make time for an old buddy. You know, bro code and all."

Elaine half-laughed, shaking her head slightly as she peered back at her chaotic calendar. "Ironically, you're lucky you don't have an actual appointment because it would have been canceled. I've been playing musical chairs with his schedule all morning."

Elaine added, "His office is a zoo back there today—electricians, handymen, you name it. Joel clocked out early."

I rolled my eyes and sucked my teeth, "Damn, just my luck, huh? Guess I'll catch him tomorrow."

She paused, thumbing through her tablet with a frown. "Hold up, tomorrow's… yeah, Thursday. Joel's off playing big brother in Camden all day. Won't catch him then."

I joked, "Saint Joel is always everywhere but here, at church events, out there saving the world, anything but taking care of us." Elaine smirked as I drummed my fingers on the counter. "So, what's the word for Friday?" I asked.

Elaine's smirk blossomed into a smile. "After lunch good for you? If you swing by, I'll sneak you in."

"Bet." I nodded. I was already plotting. With Joel off the grid tomorrow, it was prime time for Kay to do her thing.

I winked, easing off from the desk. "You're a real one, Elaine. I won't forget that when I'm king of this castle." Elaine smiled.

I swaggered back through the swinging doors, the noise from the shop floor hitting me like an old rival. Every step felt sharper than the last as I mapped out the blueprint of my next move in my plan.

*She fell into his eyes like deep water—
by the time she surfaced, she was already on her knees.*

CHAPTER THIRTY-THREE

THE KEY AND KAY

It was Thursday, May 27th, 2021, 12:07 P.M., when I leapt through those big-ass swinging doors. The second floor greeted me with an eerie quiet—no buzzing phones, no Elaine tapping away behind the desk. The whole place felt like it was holding its breath, just for me. Perfect.

My boots hit the concrete, each step echoing down the empty corridor like a countdown. At the back, past the rows of empty desks, sat Kay, hunched over her workstation, looking like she'd rather be anywhere else but there.

Our eyes locked. Hers screamed fear. Mine... pure determination.

She slid back in her chair so fast it let out a squeak, like the damn thing was snitching on her. Her shaky hand dipped into her desk drawer and pulled out the key to Joel's office—our golden ticket.

Kay stood, her steps slow and uneven; the key gripped so tight I half-expected it to bend under the pressure.

I closed the distance between us, leaning in close, close enough for her to catch the scent of my cologne. With my signature smirk locked and loaded, I let my eyes do the work—commanding, coaxing. "Deep breath, Kay," I whispered, my voice steady and low. "This isn't just for me; this is for us. Jackie's gone now; it's just you and me."

"Trust the plan." I said. "We've talked about this at least a hundred times, plus you know his office. "You've got this." I dipped my head to more tightly lock my gaze. I said, "I'll be right here, guarding the door. If I see or hear anything, I'll tap on the glass or give you a signal."

Her hands trembled as she held the key, the metal swinging in the air. I never broke eye contact, letting my amber eyes work their magic—a tool I've come to rely on.

Something shifted within her like magic, a visible change as if a soldier was snapping to attention under my command. I'd seen it before, that look when a bitch falls under what I call "The Santé Effect."

To ensure everything went smoothly, I sealed our pact with a soft kiss on her lips. "Let's do this," I murmured, reinforcing our mission with a blend of reassurance and command. Completely under my influence, Kay moved with a newfound purpose, sliding the key into Joel's door and disappearing inside.

Left alone in the hallway, I tugged at my dick, which was half hard from the excitement of it all. Every second stretched into eternity. The building's old bones creaked, throwing out sounds that broke the quiet, reminding me this place had been through some shit.

Time crawled by, thick with tension, until Joel's office door finally cracked open again. Kay stepped out, her face flipping from anxious to quiet victory.

"Done," she said, her voice a triumphant whisper.

"Done?" I echoed, letting the word hang in the air.

Her nod was firm; all business. "Done—get ready, Mr. Shop Supervisor."

A rush of exhilaration surged through me. I pulled her into a brief, fierce hug, a moment of celebration in the quiet corridor. Remembering the last detail, I broke away. "Lock his door," I instructed crisply.

Kay turned the key in the lock with a confident twist. The click of the lock was like music, a sweet note of victory. Every move, every risk, every moment of doubt had led to this—and we had nailed it.

CHAPTER THIRTY-FOUR

REFLECTIONS AND RED SILK

Wrapped in the comforting embrace of my fresh pink terry-cloth robe, my auburn hair hung damp and wild around my shoulders, still carrying the warm scent of gardenia from my shower. The dim overhead light cast a soft glow on the rose petals printed across my bed sheets, their delicate patterns dancing faintly in the quiet air of my bedroom.

The scene felt serene, almost too serene for the storm of thoughts battling inside me.

It was Saturday night, and the stakes couldn't have been higher. At precisely 8 P.M., Isaac would call with news that could shape the trajectory of our careers. Yet, at the very same time, I was expected at Santé's. Two moments, two paths, pulling at me with equal intensity.

I sat on the edge of my bed, my thoughts wrestling with each other. The logical, grounded part of me knew the significance of Isaac's call and the potential doors it could open. But another part—a side that was harder to define—was drawn to Santé and the dangerous allure he carried with him. A spark of anticipation mingled with unease, leaving me restless.

I grabbed my phone and tapped out a message:

> Running behind on my workload.

Then, without second-guessing, I added:

> Can we push things back to 9 P.M.?

My eyes drifted to the walk-in closet, a haven of fabrics and memories. Inside, I picked out a red lace-tied maxi dress, the silk cool against my fingertips. I laid it gently across the bed and chose clear-strap stilettos to pair with it—deliberate, confident choices.

Then came the jewelry. My fingers brushed over small ruby-dangling earrings, pulling them from their resting place. The deep red stones caught the dim light, evoking whispers of old dreams and secrets from a time when I wore them with a different purpose.

As if caught in a current, I opened a small box hidden at the back of my closet. Inside was a faded framed photograph of a young Latino man. His gray eyes, warm and familiar, looked back at me. A man from my past, his face still etched in my heart. I traced the outline of his smile with a finger as a single tear slipped free. The emotions stirred by the picture lingered like the faint scent of gardenia still clinging to me.

The beep of my phone brought me back to the present. Santé's reply flashed on the screen:

> Would love to see you earlier, but I'll be patient if I must. Just don't make a habit of keeping me waiting.

A small smile crept across my face. I typed back a playful reply:

> Okay.

I added a kissing emoji, as much for my own reassurance as his.

The evening loomed ahead, a careful balance of past and present, logic and longing. As I prepared for the night, the pieces of myself—the woman I was, the professional I'd become, and the one being drawn into Santé's enigmatic orbit—felt more tangled than ever.

It was a collision of choices that would ripple far beyond a quiet Saturday night.

8 P.M., DOWNSTAIRS, THE FAMILIAR PURPLE WALLS OF MY OFFICE NOOK enclosed me, offering a semblance of comfort. As I pulled up the manuscript on my laptop computer, the screen from my desktop flashed to life with Isaac's call on Skype.

"It's Good to see you chose wisely, Amanda," Isaac said, his tone threading the line between joking and painfully serious. "I was worried about Santé derailing our plans." A note of relief in his voice made me smile weakly. He added, "You know Santé can't call the shots, right?"

I played nervously with a pen on my desk, twisting it between my fingers. "I've always got my priorities in order, remember that," I responded. Feeling the weight of Isaac's scrutiny through the screen, I shifted in my seat. "I haven't spoken to him since last Saturday." I lied, avoiding Isaac's penetrating gaze.

Behind Isaac, his apartment's unmistakable beige and teal accents were visible, along with a few stray suitcases indicating his recent return from California. Sensing my unease or perhaps sensing my dishonesty on the issue, Isaac tilted his head slightly, his gaze scrutinizing. "You haven't spoken to him at all?"

Clearing my throat, I swiftly refocused the conversation: "About the book, Isaac. Are we moving forward?"

Isaac's eyebrows raised, but his face revealed a hint of amusement. "Funny you should ask. The L.A. trip was... eye opening."

I leaned forward, my anticipation evident. "What do you mean?"

Isaac rolled his eyes before explaining, "The studio executives suggested I get a job inside television. They said having an internal perspective, in addition to forming my own production company, would make a big difference. Funny, right?"

My fingers tapped the desk, betraying my impatience. "Going Hollywood, is that something you're considering?"

Isaac gave a noncommittal shrug. "Maybe. If it leads to the right doors opening, why not? But for now, I have bigger news."

My heart raced. "Tell me."

Isaac started his slow rollout, "Well, while L.A. didn't yield a concrete movie deal, I've got something for you."

My palms felt wet with sweat. "Go on..." I said.

Isaac started slowly, "I pitched the 'Santé's Secrets' concept as a film or television project, and they liked the idea. But when I told them it would be a book first, they loved it even more. They said it would be a more valuable film property if fans already liked it as a book."

Isaac teased, "And well..."

Rocking in my chair, I demanded, "Well what, Isaac?"

He smirked, seemingly loving my anticipation; he said, "Mr. Jacobs made a few calls to a few publishing houses, and sis-boom-bah, they loved it!" He exclaimed, "We've got a publishing deal."

"Wait, what?" I blinked rapidly, my mind racing to keep up. "They may want to make a publishing deal?"

Isaac grinned. "Even better, the deal's done," he announced, his grin infectious. "Just sign the papers, and the $10,000 advance is yours."

Elated, I jumped up, my chair scraping back. Suddenly, I was dancing around my office nook like it was a stage.

Isaac laughed, but his expression quickly sobered. "Okay, let's rein it in. We've got work to do! But first, your feelings?" Isaac asked, always the protective one.

"I'm on cloud nine," I replied, my voice breathy with excitement.

Isaac leaned in, his face serious yet supportive. "Amanda, this is huge. If you're not 100% in, I need to know now. This isn't just about you; it's about both of us."

Determined, I replied, "Send the contract. I'll sign it right away."

Isaac seemed reassured. "Full steam ahead then?"

My fist clenched in resolve, I replied, "Full steam ahead. No turning back."

Isaac leaned even closer to the camera, his intensity palpable through the screen. "This book, Amanda... I read what you've done with the manuscript so far; it's magnificent, hun. I can see the work you've put into it."

Isaac's voice softened, his eyes slightly moist. "It's got the potential to launch us both. Your mix of over the top freaky sex, subtle sexual allure, life lessons, and heartbreak, women will see themselves in it."

Humbled, I nodded. "Thank you, Isaac. I promise, the finished manuscript will be ready in two weeks."

A genuine smile spread across Isaac's face. "Then I guess you have a deal."

I replied with tearful emotion, "No, *we* have a deal. I love you, friend."

Eyes wet and glistening, Isaac whispered, "I love you Judy-girl."

The call ended, and Isaac's face vanished from the screen, leaving me with the afterglow of exhilarating news.

The gravity of what just transpired hit me. I took a deep breath, letting the magnitude of the news sink in. My eyes wandered to an old picture of Isaac and me from our college days, both of us laughing at some long-forgotten joke.

This was an image of the distance traveled from our college days, where we had debated our very different dreams for our lives over cheap coffee, to now, sealing the unity of this publishing deal.

I thought it was incredible how far we'd come. The emotional high was immense, but in that quiet moment, I was also grounded in the bedrock of gratitude and history.

Then, a spark of realization: My Saturday night was not yet over; next door, Santé Sabatino awaited.

*She fell into his eyes like deep water—
by the time she surfaced, she was already on her knees.*

CHAPTER THIRTY-FIVE

LADY IN RED

The hidden cameras upstairs were rolling; I made damn sure of it before heading down the stairs. Halfway down, my phone chimed. Amanda's message popped up: *"Crossing the lawn in two minutes."*

I glanced at the clock: 8:59. I smirked, muttering, "So she'll be here by 9:01." Not bad, considering she's already an hour late.

I hustled into the living room, double-checking the hidden camera and mic I'd set up earlier. "Hope this shit works," I muttered, imagining Amanda spilling all her dirty little secrets.

The kitchen called next. I tossed shrimp-loaded meat sauce into one bowl and some basic pasta into another. Plates, silverware, the whole nine yards—all set on the folding table like I was serving at a damn five-star restaurant.

"Looking good," I said to myself, admiring my setup.

The takeout bags got dumped fast and quiet. No need for Amanda to figure out where the food really came from. A grin crept across my face as I shot to the front door, unlocked it, and rushed back to the living room.

I plopped down on the couch, flicked on the big screen, and dimmed the volume just enough. My bare feet pressed against the cool gray and white wood floors, grounding me while I prepped for the night's performance.

"Stay calm, Santé," I whispered, smoothing my blue button-up against my chest. It was snug, sticking to my back. I had light sweat from all the running around, but my jeans fit like a glove, giving me just enough room for my semi-hard dick.

When Amanda walked in, all that prep felt worth it. "Damn," I thought, my eyes dragging over her red maxi dress. The lace-up sides? Sexy as hell. My dick got harder and my jeans got tighter just looking at her.

I stood to greet her, my voice smooth. "Welcome inside my home for the first time."

Her smile matched her tone—classy, but warm. "Thank you for the invitation and your patience."

Patience? That dress could've made a saint lose his. Her auburn curls shimmered under the overhead lights, and when she leaned in for a quick hug, my lips brushed her cheek. Her scent—warm gardenia—hit me, stirring something deeper.

She clocked the food right away. "I knew I smelled something delicious when I walked through the door," she teased.

I grinned. "Thanks for the compliment. What you smell is absolutely delicious. The food's probably good too."

Her blush was subtle but real. "Is that Eros by Versace?"

"Absolutely," I said.

She tilted her head. "You cooked?"

I laughed. "Hey, you saw me at the cookout, right?"

"That's grilling. This is cuisine," she shot back, a sly grin curling her lips.

I pushed my chest out. "Never underestimate me."

Her eyes lingered on the plates. "How did you know I like pasta?"

"It was a gamble," I admitted. "Especially with the shrimp in the meat sauce. You're not allergic, are you?"

She shook her head with a smile. "No, I actually enjoy shrimp."

"Good," I said, letting my eyes roam over her dress again. "That shade of red? Beautiful." The words slipped out before I could reel them back.

Amanda's smile deepened. That's when it hit me—a crazy idea, something I'd normally laugh off—romance.

I moved to the wall near the TV, fumbling through my surround sound system. Found the track faster than I expected. Amanda stood, curiosity lighting up her face.

I hit play and turned back toward her, my hand extended. "Before we eat," I said, my voice low and steady, "would you do me the honor of one dance?"

Chris de Burgh's *Lady in Red* spilled from the speakers, the timing too perfect to be anything but fate.

Her face flushed as red as her dress, but she took my hand. I pulled her close, our bodies swaying to the slow rhythm. Cheek to cheek, we moved in small circles, her warmth pressing into me in all the right ways.

For a moment, I let myself feel something I hadn't felt in years—tenderness. Not since Jackie had I let this side of me out. Victoria never got this version of me. She was hooked on the rough edges, the chaos. But Amanda? She was different. Before I let the beast out, I wanted her to see the knight in shining armor buried deep.

We danced through the entire song, then swayed in silence for a while longer. Her scent, her softness—it was all working on me.

But as the moment faded, so did the tenderness. The cameras were rolling, and I had plans to fuck on film.

"Alright," I said, pulling back just enough to look into her eyes. "Let's eat."

CHAPTER THIRTY-SIX

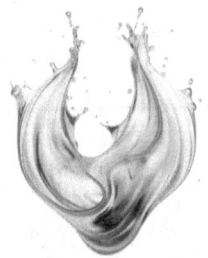

SEDUCTION BREAKS THROUGH

Amanda was practically breathless, still caught up in the spell of our dance. She might've been soaking in the romance, but I was already a few moves ahead, setting the stage for what came next.

I gestured toward the living room, where I'd set up dinner. "I figured the living room works for tonight. Hope you don't mind skipping the formal dining room."

Her smile came easy, and her eyes lit up as she moved toward the table. "Not at all," she said, her voice soft. "I'm just impressed you cooked for me. And that dance? It felt... magical."

I grinned, letting her eat it up. "I'm glad you enjoyed it. Let's see if the food lives up to the hype."

Of course, I knew damn well Angelo's Italian had done the heavy lifting. But the way she was looking at me, she'd never suspect I'd outsourced dinner.

We sat down and ate mostly in silence, her eyes flicking to me now and then like she was studying me. I didn't mind the attention. Hell, I thrived on it. But as the meal went on, I decided it was time to shake things up.

I leaned back casually, twirling my fork in the last bit of pasta. "You know, for all the time we've spent together, I realized something," I said, letting the words hang in the air just long enough to get her attention.

Amanda glanced up mid-bite, her eyebrows lifting slightly. "What's that?"

"I don't really know much about you," I said, my tone light but pointed.

Her giggle was soft, almost nervous, and she covered her mouth as she swallowed. "What do you want to know?"

I tilted my head, studying her reaction. "Anything. But there is one thing I've been curious about."

Her hand hovered near her wineglass, and I didn't miss the slight tremble in her fingers. "Like what?" she asked, her voice dipping a little.

I leaned forward, keeping my eyes locked on hers. "Seems like every time we're together, I'm spilling all my wildest stories. Even that five-dollar game—it was all about me. Why is that?"

Her fingers tightened on the stem of her wineglass, and she avoided my gaze. "Your stories," she started, her voice not quite steady, "they're captivating. I guess I just wanted to understand you better."

I wasn't buying it. "Captivating, huh? But why the freaky ones? There were plenty of other stories I could've shared, but you kept pushing for the wildest ones."

She hesitated, her fingers fidgeting with the wine glass like it held all her answers. "I suppose they're just... more revealing. They show a different side of you."

I raised an eyebrow, leaning in just enough to keep the pressure on. "And what side is that?"

Her lips parted slightly, but instead of answering, she picked up the wineglass and took a long sip. A classic stalling move. I let her have her moment, but I wasn't about to let her dodge me forever.

When she finally put the glass down, her voice was softer, more careful. "People's wildest stories say a lot about them. Their fears, their desires..."

I smirked. "So it's all curiosity, then? Nothing more?"

She didn't answer right away, her eyes drifting to the bottle of Chardonnay. I nodded toward it. "Go ahead," I said, watching her every move. The way her hands trembled slightly, the way her eyes avoided mine—it all told me she was hiding something.

After another sip, she finally spoke. "Some things are better left unsaid, Santé."

Her words were careful, but I could see she was cracking. I pushed a little harder. "Amanda, I've been an open book with you. Why can't you do the same?"

Her fingers traced the rim of the glass, her gaze distant. "It's not that simple. There's more at stake here than you realize."

I leaned in, my voice low and firm. "Whatever it is, you can trust me."

She looked at me then, really looked at me, and for a moment, I thought she might finally spill. But instead, she sighed and said, "I told you, I used to be a therapist. I guess I just like listening to people's stories. It's... therapeutic."

Bullshit. I could see right through her. But I played it cool, letting her think she'd dodged me. "Fair enough," I said, leaning back in my seat. "But it's interesting—listening to my nastiest stories doesn't seem to bother you at all."

She didn't respond, and I knew I'd hit a nerve. Whatever game Amanda was playing, it was big. Bigger than she wanted me to know. And if she thought she could outsmart me, she had another think coming.

I shifted gears, letting the tension settle before I made my next move.

Glancing at her now-empty plate, I offered, "Would you like seconds?"

Amanda looked surprised, seemingly unaware she'd finished her meal. She took a moment to survey the almost empty serving bowls and then gently declined, "No, thank you. The meal was delicious."

I shifted in my seat, pulling myself upright. "I truly enjoy the moments we spend together, but I'm torn. I'm grappling with my feelings for you and this undeniable attraction."

A subtle smile formed on Amanda's lips. "Attraction?"

Taking another breath, I feigned courage and admitted, "I didn't just invite you over for a simple dinner. I also wanted this evening to display how much I... I desire you."

Amanda opened her mouth, then hesitated, her eyes flickering toward her wine glass. I could see she was trying to process my words, maybe even question my sincerity. But I kept going.

"I didn't think I'd ever feel like this again, not after Jackie," I said, letting the name hang in the air like bait. "After what happened... I thought I'd walled off that part of me for good. But with you... it's like those walls don't even exist."

Amanda's lips parted a bit, and for a moment, I thought she might speak, but she stayed quiet. Her hand trembled slightly as she reached for the wine bottle, pouring herself another glass. The silence between us stretched, and I let it. Sometimes, silence did more work than words.

Finally, she spoke, her voice soft. "It's not easy to let those walls down, Santé."

Her fingers traced the rim of her glass, her gaze distant. "I... I thought I'd done the same thing. Told myself I'd never open up like that again." She paused, swallowing hard. "But sometimes, life doesn't let you keep those promises."

I leaned in, my eyes locking onto hers. "What'da ya mean?" I asked, keeping my voice steady, low, drawing her in.

Her eyes flickered with something—pain, maybe. Regret. "He..." She stopped herself, shaking her head.

I stayed quiet, watching her carefully. Amanda wasn't the type to give up personal details easily, so whatever this was, it had her rattled.

"He had these gray eyes. I swear they could see straight through me." She began, her voice steady but distant. "He was so... alive. Every laugh, every word—it felt like he brought the world to life around him."

She hesitated, her fingers gripping the wine glass tighter. "Sometimes, I catch myself thinking about him when I least expect it. Like he's still here, just... out of reach." Her voice was shaky, but she pulled herself together quickly.

The way she spoke told me enough. This wasn't just any ex; this was someone who had got to her, left his mark—deep, and she was still carrying it, whether she admitted it or not.

"That's why I told myself I wouldn't..." She cut herself off, shaking her head. "I wouldn't do this again. It's safer that way."

Safer. That was the word she used. I softened my tone, leaning in closer. "You're safe with me," I said, letting the words roll off my tongue like a promise. "I'm not asking you to fill anything, Amanda. I'm just asking you to trust me. To let me in, one step at a time."

Her lip trembled slightly, and she took a shaky breath. For a second, I thought I saw her walls come down just a bit, and I knew I had to move quickly.

Pulling back to my side of the couch, I let the tension that had started to slip away build back up as I paused.

"Look, Amanda," I began slowly, "I've got something else to say, something I've been holding onto."

Suddenly, there was a shift in Amanda. The vulnerability that had been on display only moments ago was tucked away as she sat up straighter, her chin lifting slightly higher.

"And... what is that?" she asked, her tone blending authority and genuine interest.

"I think I'm falling for you," I admitted, looking carefully for her reaction.

She looked thoughtful. "You mentioned that last week. But what exactly do you mean?"

I sighed, choosing my words carefully. "I mean, I'm catching feelings. Real ones. Look, after my divorce, I put up walls around my heart. But with you, they're all coming down. I think I can trust again."

With puppy-dog eyes, I added, "I need to know if you feel the same for me as I do for you. I don't want to waste your time or mine."

Amanda listened carefully to my every word, but her eyes were locked on the remainder of her food. She immediately shoveled it into her mouth, delaying her response.

With my last spoonful of patience, I waited for her to swallow the remaining strands of spaghetti, heavily covered with meat sauce.

With a deep breath and avoiding my eyes again, Amanda spoke softly, "It's been a long time since I've felt this way, but every day I find myself getting closer to you."

I nodded, faking empathy. I said, "Of course. I'm sorry if I'm moving too fast."

Clearing my throat, I leaned in closer to her. "Look... the rest of the evening... it's really up to you."

Amanda looked at me, a hint of confusion evident in her eyes. "I'm not sure what you mean."

I took a deep breath and feigned courage, admitting, "I didn't just invite you over for a simple dinner. I also wanted this evening to display how much I... I desire you."

I then rose from my seat, figuring my intentions were clear. "Look, I won't pressure you. It's just not my style. If you want me as much as I want you, I'll be in my bedroom. It's upstairs, the large room to the left. If you don't want to join me, I'll understand. Just make sure the door's locked on your way out; once you're done with your wine."

Before Amanda could speak, I leaned down, gently pressing my lips against hers. "Regardless of what you decide, just know how special you are to me."

I strolled away from Amanda, each step of my bare feet a seductive tease. As I climbed the stairs, I could feel a sly grin forming on my face. I knew my power, and I was positive that pussy was mine.

Reaching the top step, I slowly unbuttoned my shirt. I was confident that I was gonna fuck Amanda that night. Entering my bedroom, concealed with video surveillance, only one sound punctured the silence: the unzipping of my jeans.

CHAPTER THIRTY-SEVEN

ALL CRASHED DOWN

I pushed through those familiar swinging doors to the second floor, expecting the usual back and forth, low-key flirting with Elaine, but something was off. Elaine was on the phone, flustered as hell. "It's happening now." she said, her eyes darting to the wall clock. I followed her eyes—1 P.M., my scheduled time with Joel.

Elaine gestured for me to head straight to the back offices. I nodded, feeling the pressure. "Thanks, Elaine.", I said, but she completely ignored me.

My pace quickened. But as I headed down the side hall, I could tell something was wrong. Muffled yelling and crying were getting louder with every step closer to Joel's office.

When I passed by Kay's workspace, she was MIA, but Trina and Yvette were sitting there, trying to look busy while clearly eavesdropping on the drama oozing out of Joel's office. They avoided eye contact, sneaking glances at me.

Curious, I turned to Yvette. "What's going down in Joel's office?"

She started with, "Child..." but whatever she was gonna say next got swallowed up by the full volume of shouts and sobs as Joel's door swung open.

"You know how much I hate lies and liars! Both abominations!" Joel's voice cut through the sounds of crying like a knife.

Kay stumbled out, tears streaming down her face. "Why won't you give me a chance to explain?"

Joel wasn't having it. "What's there to explain? I showed you the video. Even Lee saw it."

Lee popped up behind Kay, adding his two cents, "I was shocked, Kay. It wasn't like you."

She snapped back, "Would you shut up, Lee? This ain't about you."

But Joel wasn't letting up. "What do you mean, not about Lee? You altered his performance reviews."

Instinctively, I took a step back, knowing the jig was up. My feet wanted to backtrack all the way down the hall, out to the reception area, and bolt down the front steps. But before I could make my move, Joel's keen eye caught me.

"Santé?" His voice was a mix of surprise and irritation.

I froze mid-step, feeling their stares burning into me.

Kay's eyes, wet and desperate, locked onto mine, silently begging me to vouch for her. But all I could manage was a hesitant, "I-I can come back later."

Lee shot me a suspicious look, while Joel, a bit more understanding, said, "Oh, Santé, there's no need."

Dread washed over me. Images of unemployment and bankruptcy flashed before my eyes.

Then shit got worse, Kay pleaded, "Santé, would you please say something?"

Fuck! My bitch was about to dime me out, I thought. Fucked for sure.

Lee's eyes look through me like an X-ray. I just knew the jig was up.

But in that split second of hesitation, Joel started laying it all out. "Kay, I've suspected you've been breaking into my office for some time now."

Kay gasped, "What?"

Joel laid it out plain and simple. "Kay, you're one of the two people with keys to my office—Elaine and you. My office has been messed with too many times. Papers shuffled, items misplaced, lights left on. But the final straw was the last break-in. My Super Jenga tower was destroyed, left in pieces, and you didn't even bother to pick them up. That's when I had the new lights and surveillance installed."

Kay shot me a look of pure defeat.

Joel wasn't done. "And that's also when I decided the culprit had to be caught, fired, maybe even prosecuted."

The word prosecuted echoed in my head, a sudden headache threatening to split my skull.

Kay's voice quivered, "Fired? I'm done?"

Joel's response was cold and final. "Absolutely done. I'm done with you, Kay. You're fired. Effective immediately." Then he turned to me. "Now, as for you, Santé…"

I braced myself, fully expecting to get axed next. But Joel just said, "No need for our meeting. Lee's the new supervisor."

Kay's gaze slowly shifted from Joel to me, pure anger in her eyes.

Lee was all smiles, thanking Joel, while the tension in the hallway hit a breaking point. I decided to make a hasty exit.

"That's what's up. Congratulations, Lee. Joel, I'll be down on the floor," I said, eager to get the fuck out of there.

I made a mad dash for the swinging doors, practically leaping down the front steps.

Elaine's voice floated after me, and I couldn't bring myself to respond to her most ironic words, "Enjoy the rest of your day, Santé."

*She fell into his eyes like deep water—
by the time she surfaced, she was already on her knees.*

CHAPTER THIRTY-EIGHT

DRENCHED AND DISORIENTED

The darkness was impenetrable, like the depths of an ocean at midnight. Suddenly, strobe lights flashed, slicing through the void with erratic bursts of white light. I blinked, disoriented, as the shadows and light played tricks on my eyes, making it hard to discern what was real and what wasn't.

I found myself walking on campus, clutching my diploma. The cap and gown weighed heavily on my shoulders, a symbol of accomplishment. The familiar pathways of my university felt surreal in the dream's haze. I made my way towards the dorms, but as I entered the building, an eerie stillness greeted me. The usually bustling halls were silent and empty, devoid of life.

"Bridge Over Troubled Water," a voice echoed faintly. The words seemed to float in the air, carried by an unseen presence. I walked down the empty halls, the sound of my footsteps amplified in the silence. The voice repeated the phrase, each time growing a little louder, a little clearer.

At the end of the hallway, I reached a door. Pushing it open, I stepped into an alley. The transition was abrupt and jarring. The alley was narrow, with high brick walls on either side. Darkness cloaked the path ahead, and I felt a sense of foreboding. The sky above was overcast, heavy with impending rain.

As I walked further, the first drops of rain began to fall, quickly turning into a downpour. My cap and gown were soon soaked, clinging to my skin. I hugged my diploma to my chest, trying to shield it from the relentless rain. The ink on the paper started to smudge, the edges curling under the moisture.

"Amanda, I'm not sick anymore." My mother's voice called out, clear and strong. I froze, my heart pounding in my chest. I hadn't heard my mother's voice so clearly since before the cancer. Her voice was filled with a warmth and vitality I hadn't heard in years. Tears mingled with the rain on my face, blurring my vision. I wanted to call out to her, but my voice was lost in the storm.

Gunshots rang out, sharp and piercing, cutting through the rain's rhythm. I flinched, my body tensing in fear. The alley seemed to close in around me, the walls pressing tighter. "Save me, Amanda." A male voice pleaded, filled with desperation. The rain intensified, pounding against the pavement, drowning out the surrounding sounds. But the voice persisted, growing louder, more insistent.

"Save me, Amanda!"

Lightning split the sky with a blinding flash, followed by the deafening roar of thunder. The alley was momentarily illuminated, revealing dark figures lurking in the shadows. Panic surged through me as I tried to make sense of the chaos. The lightning struck again, closer this time, its jagged streak slicing through the air.

I jolted awake, my body drenched in sweat. My bedroom felt both familiar and foreign as I tried to shake off the remnants of the dream. The dim overhead light cast a gentle glow, creating soft shadows on the walls. My comforter, adorned with rose petals, was twisted around me, a tangled mess from my restless sleep. It was a shock—I hadn't had a dream like that in many years.

I sat up, running a hand through my damp hair, my heart still racing. The vivid images from the dream lingered in my mind—the empty halls, the alley, the rain, my late mother's voice, and the desperate plea for help. As a degreed psychologist, I hoped my understanding of the principles of psychology would give me insight into what the meaning of this dream was. Unfortunately, my educational pedigree did little to help me make the connections that I knew were there.

Why was I having this dream? Why had the dreams that used to haunt me as a young adult returned? My mind replayed the scenes over and over, each detail etched into my memory, but the meaning remained elusive. The lingering sense of unease was impossible to dismiss.

I lay back down, staring at the ceiling, the gentle light soothing me. The dream had felt so real, so intense, that it was hard to believe it was just a figment of my subconscious. What did it all mean? The question echoed in my thoughts as I slowly drifted back into a restful sleep, hoping for answers.

CHAPTER THIRTY-NINE

A POOL OF TROUBLE

The full moon hung high, its glow casting spooky silver shadows over the lone Buick in the parking lot. Monday afternoon's failures and fuckery had rattled my spirit and shaken my confidence, leaving me restless and wired. All day, the Swim Club whispered to me, its pull magnetic, its promise intoxicating. It called to me like the temptation of a bitch's thighs, impossible to resist.

By 10:05 P.M., I couldn't fight it anymore. I turned the key, stepping into the silent, empty club. Drawn to the water like a moth to a flame, I felt its soothing promise even before the first splash. My first stop—the single shower just feet from the pool's edge.

The warm water slid over my chest, calming my restless energy, and cascading down my balls to my bare feet. My routine was automatic now: get inside, get naked, get wet, and get into the pool.

Under the dim, half-lit pool lights, the water shimmered like liquid crystal, reflecting my image. I wiggled my toes against the cool tile, sucking in a deep breath before leaping in. The impact broke the glass-like surface, bubbles scrambling upward as I sliced through the water, each stroke deliberate, and powerful.

Lap after lap, my body moved on autopilot, but my mind drifted, seduced by a familiar mental slip. The strokes of my arms and the kick of my legs—all of it faded into the background as my thoughts painted vivid images. Scenes of conquest and seduction lit up in my mind, as if the water unlocked the gates to my most freaky memories.

No longer in the pool, I was back in my kingdom, an instant replay of last weekend's after-dinner action with Amanda. I was naked, hard, and sitting on my bed, lying back a bit.

Amanda's silhouette filled the doorway, her curves framed by the soft glow of the hallway light. She hesitated for a second, her breath halting as her eyes locked on my dick, widening in surprise, or maybe awe.

"Geesh," she whispered, her voice low and breathy, like she was trying to wrap her head around what she saw—my rock-hard dick standing at attention.

I smirked and rose, motioning for her to come closer. Her movements were cautious, her steps slow, deliberate, as if some invisible line had been drawn in the carpet, and crossing it meant surrendering to whatever I demanded. She paused just out of reach, her eyes darting up and down my body.

She called my name breathlessly; "Santé! "

I put my index finger to my lips. "Shhh." Once I had her attention, I said, "Talking time is over, baby."

I lumbered over to her with the grace and power of a lion. I leaned forward and peered at her intensely as my hands gripped her shoulders firmly. Amanda seemed hypnotized by the swirling spectrum in my eyes and oblivious to the pressure of my hands on her shoulders. I guided her down the slow descent to the thick gray rug that stretched out before the bed.

She followed obediently, her eyes fixed on me, still mesmerized. Her auburn curls framed her sexy face, catching a key light from the bedside lamp. I tilted my head back briefly, scanning the pinholes in the ceiling and walls, ensuring everything was in position. The thought of the freaky shit those cameras were about to capture made my dick jump. Glancing back down, Amanda's eyes flared.

"Don't be scared now, baby," I challenged. My fingers traced the outline of her upper and lower lips. "Suck me, Manda," I whispered.

Looking up at me, Amanda's hands hesitated for a moment, hovering near my thighs before she committed. "You know you want that dick, girl." I said, moaning. She touched my meat lightly at first. Her lips followed, soft and warm—she was captured.

Amanda's tongue's careful exploration of the head of my dick quickly grew bolder, taking me further into her mouth.

I leaned back, letting her find her rhythm. The heat of her mouth sent waves of pleasure that rippled through me. Her movements were unpracticed but genuine, each hesitant touch a reminder that I was in control, shaping the dick suck exactly as I wanted it.

Soon Amanda's hungry mouth tried to take more inches down her throat. I secretly made eye contact with the cameras, glancing down into Amanda's eyes now and then—keeping her attention on me.

Her pace quickened, and soon I began jamming the dick into her mouth. Spreading my fingers through her hair, my grip firm and masculine. "Come to Papi, bitch," I growled. The sensation was electric, her eagerness obvious, her nose just inches from my belly, bouncing towards my body like she was captured by some magnetic force.

As the water from my swim splashed, the sex movie with Amanda played in my mind's eye with crystal clarity. Me fucking Amanda's mouth with greater energy. She was completely unaware that I was guiding her dick-stuffed face into multiple camera angles.

I could feel the back of her throat on the head of my 'Puerto Rican Python'. The vibrations as she gagged, the drool on my balls—I loved it all.

Before long I was inside her pussy. Amanda's hair fanned out against the gray, thick comforter as I leaned over her, dicking her deep. "Oh shit, that's it, that's it.", she cried.

I liked that she was enjoying the dick, but it was obvious she needed training for the proper protocol. "That's it—who bitch?" I dug three more inches deep. Amanda's pussy quivered as she screamed, "That's it, Papi!—That's it, Papi!"

A cocky grin formed on my face, and I looked directly at one of the pinholes in the wall as I said, "That's right, bitch... It's Papi to you, and don't forget it." I followed my lesson with a light hand slap across her face.

Her cheeks immediately flushed, the one I slapped plus the other one. A faint pink spread down her neck too. She groaned deep as hell.

I watched the nervous rise and fall of her chest, her cherry-brown eyes wild, and her breath panting like a bitch in heat.

The tension in her body spoke volumes—hesitation, excitement, surrender—all dancing together in contradiction and yet, in perfect harmony.

I traced the edge of her soft jaw with the back of my fingers; she flinched, expecting another slap. Pounding her pussy with more force and swivel from my hips, I let my touch linger just long enough to leave her wanting more.

I could feel the spongy part of her pussy swelling and the occasional muscle spasms of her creamy walls. She wanted to cum, but she was holding back. She was probably overwhelmed by the intensity.

Every day simps never fucked Amanda like I was fucking her. So I sensed she needed permission to get lost. She was holding back, trying to keep her soul.

Too bad for her, she was playing with the wrong motherfucker; no bitch had ever left my bed without me collecting her soul. Her deceitful ass was not going to be the first.

I turned up the heat, leaning in, my lips finding hers, tasting the faint crispness of the Chardonnay we'd shared earlier. Her arms slid around my neck, pulling me closer, her nails grazing my shoulders as our breaths mingled.

Her pussy jumped more often and faster than the beat of my stroke. She was close to a hell of a release, but she was still soul-clutching.

"You don't have to hold back," I murmured, then whispered, "Not here. Not with me. Not with Santé."

With my voice and name still lingering in the air, I deep dicked Amanda's pussy like I was drilling for oil. Her lips parted slightly as if she wanted to speak, but no words came. Instead, her hands found their way to my back, her fingernails clawed my skin as she let out a high-decibel howl.

"I'm... I'm Cummin' Papi", her voice shaky and disoriented.

Despite her grip on my back, there was a softness to her touch, a vulnerability I had been waiting for. It wasn't just desire anymore—it was trust, raw and real, unmistakable in the way her body convulsed beneath mine. She was separating. Santé's spell was striking again, and it couldn't be happening to a more deserving bitch. After three or four minutes, Amanda took a deep breath and exhaled slowly.

Then it happened — the moment I had been waiting for, the event I wanted from all of my bitches—her soul escaped her body and entered mine. I felt the familiar release, the subtle electrical charge.

For a moment, the world narrowed to just that instant—her warmth, her scent, the way she melted around me—she was mine.

The cameras above caught everything, but right then, I wasn't thinking about them. Not entirely. It was just us, tangled in a rhythm, a ritual.

As I could've predicted, her energy decreased as mine soared. Even without the BDSM practices of discipline, that bitch was entering subspace from just my dick alone. Yes, she was fucking with a professional.

I could have simply worked toward my nut and ended the fuck session, but I knew she was sliding into that timeless space where I could fuck her as much as I wanted and she would willingly take the ride.

Although her mind was fading to a distant land reserved just for fuck puppies, it would be hours before her body would quit.

So for the next four hours, I fucked her doggy style. Remembering her deception, I no longer wanted to see her pretty, lying face. I just wanted to feel the quiver of her tight hot-pocket-pussy and to hear the moans of her pleasure and her occasional coochie ache.

By the end of the fourth hour, Amanda tried to run from the dick, an involuntary response to her exhaustion and extended internal stretching as my deeper dicking increased; while the night's hours decreased, slipping away.

The eleventh inch of my dick was always the toughest for bitches to take. But each time Amanda came, she opened up a little more.

During one of my many hard pussy-beatin' bursts and powerful hip rotations, Amanda came so intensely she squirted all over my sheets and her pussy walls stretched, making room for my infamous eleventh inch.

Amanda immediately weakened and fell forward, her face nestled in my gray cotton bedsheets.

But I wouldn't allow her to rest for long. As her new Puerto Rican Papi, I pulled her hair, then danced in her pulsating piñata faster—salsa style. I also wanted her face up high so at least one of my cameras could clearly see all the hardcore action; even Amanda's micro-reactions to Daddy's Dick-down.

Her asshole winked at me several times throughout the night, but I didn't take the bait. I never even made an attempt. Although she was a woman full of deception, I knew too many viewers of the sex tape would see her as a victim if I put it in her ass; it wouldn't matter whether she gave me her consent.

Video could prove she gave up the pussy, but my dick to her booty-hole would be a completely different hassle, a risk not worth the effort.

So I grabbed her tantalizing titties from underneath, squeezing her soft, large, pink nipples between my fingers; making her pussy jump, which caused my balls to tighten.

My first nut didn't arrive until forty-five minutes from our start. Amanda came countless times during our six-hour fuck-fest, but soon I felt the special sensation again.

The signal of my fourth, and what I had decided would be my final nut, arrived. I knew it was almost time for me to cum again and for her to go—possibly for good.

I looked for signs the cameras were still recording as I prepared for my close-up. In the far corner of my bedroom, I saw the small red light—everything was good.

A few minutes later, that familiar warm tingle strengthened. Her ass cheeks made clapping sounds around my dick so intense, it sounded like rounds of applause—honoring me with a prestigious award.

Amanda's booty still had the sheen from Papi's Penis potion, delivered from my first three-ass blast. But there was no way I was going to nut on her ass again.

For my finale, I wanted the power and the pleasure of painting her face with my cum. My dick was the brush, her face the canvas; art, and karma demanded no alternative ending.

I could've probably stroked her pussy a few more times, but I wasn't about to push my luck and miss delivering the perfect cum shot. So, I pulled my dick from her warm wet snatch and tapped my monster meat on her ass cheek. "Quick, turnover!" I said.

Amanda looked like she was coming out of a pleasure trance, disoriented but not disobedient; she flipped herself like a pancake. With her pretty face in front of me, and my hard dick in hand; I straddled her chest, my balls just an inch below her chin.

Confused, Amanda shook her head in caution. But before she could protest, I leaned back, making sure her face and my dick were in perfect view from all angles. Then, my toes tightened, and my cum broke free... "Uhhhhh!"—The roar rattled my room.

Even though I had cum three times before, I still bust buckets of ball juice for that bitch. I shot several shiny silver-white bullets of cum across her fucking face. Feeling the power of my domination was as delightful as my delivery—of cum.

Amanda took two shots to her left eye, her lips were fully coated and her cheeks were glazed with a priceless, protein facial—a masterpiece was made.

With her face painted white, Amanda entered my bathroom, and simultaneously she left my desire. My mission was accomplished. My body grew limp, although my dick was still hard. Laying on the bed, my mind floated.

Back in the pool, I was no longer above the waterline; I had moved close to the bottom. Running out of air, I needed to resurface. Anxiety raged as my oxygen level fell. I thought I heard a voice and perhaps a yell.

Breaking the water's surface, I inhaled sharply, the chill of fear gripping me. It wasn't just that I misjudged my air supply, but the sharp voice of some stranger cutting through, demanding answers. I whipped around toward the voice. "What the hell are you doing here, and naked for fuck's sake?" he snapped, keys jingling in his hand.

"I just arrived."—I lied.

The new manager stood there, arms crossed, bold and pissed. His dark face caught the pool lights just enough to make the man look ten feet tall. "I saw you from my Buick," he snapped. "Gave you a chance to leave. Now the cops are on their way."

Damn. No bluffing my way out of this one. My pulse shot sky-high. "Shit," I muttered under my breath. It was time to move.

I leaped out of the pool, water flying everywhere, and made a mad dash to the locker room. I grabbed enough clothes to cover my dick and balls—well, at least my balls were completely covered.

My heart was slamming so hard I thought it'd bust through my chest. I yanked on my jeans, still dripping wet, and snatched my shirt in one hand, bolting for the exit before the cops could show up and add to my already fucked up week.

Carol was gone. Her replacement? A rulebook-loving hard-ass with no chill. With her out, so was my golden ticket to the pool after hours. My spot, my sanctuary, poof—gone, just like that.

Outside, the Buick's headlights sliced through the dark like a damn searchlight, and I felt my grip on things slipping further. No promotion. No more secret pool nights. And Amanda? Who the fuck knew what her deal was.

It felt like my whole world was free-falling, unraveling piece by piece, and I didn't have a clue how to stop it. I just needed everything to slow down. Not forever—just long enough to catch my breath and figure out my next move. Damp, disrespected, and desperate, I couldn't shake one thought: What the fuck 'was' my next move?

CHAPTER FORTY

RED WALLS, STOLEN SECRETS

I had been low key for the week, but it seemed drama knew my address. I was in the kitchen when the bell rang. A quick peep into the living room and boom, Amanda's silhouette was clear as day. Thought 'bout darting upstairs, but no way was she gonna have me ducking in my own place.

I'd barely opened the door, and Amanda started with her nonsense, "You ghosted me for a whole week, Santé?" Her hand on her hip, all attitude.

I took a breath, trying to contain my rage. "Yo, I ain't open my crib for the drama, lies, or your special brand of bullshit. All that can stay on the other side of my door for real, especially after the shitshow of a week I've had.

Stepping inside, Amanda gave a snarky laugh, the kind that scraped my nerves raw. She asked, "What happened to the sharp, witty Santé I knew? Up and switched gears on me, huh?"

It took a moment for me to register her jab; I didn't react; instead, I focused my attention. "You think I'ma' let you stand there and play the victim? Nah, Amanda. We danced to the same beat, now all of a sudden you're singing a whole new tune."

She looked shaken for a minute, then acted innocent. "What are you even talking about?"

I wanted to tear into her, but my mind played tricks on me. In that instant, I became only half present; my mind raced back to her place, the countless times I spilled my guts in her red-walled lounge, sitting on her couch, every 'tell me more Santé', now echoing like a setup.

All those pieces of cake, the other home-cooked comforts, and 'you're such a deep thinker' lines felt like a hustle. Damn, every single meet-up might've been nothing but a fuckin' scam.

"What are you even talking about?" she repeated, returning me to the moment. I sneered at the false care in her voice. "Speak in a way I can understand," she said.

I ignored how she was trying to make me feel small and dumb. Or the déjà vu of the dance where she twirled around the truth. "You really got no clue?" I asked, but inside, I knew she knew the fuckin' truth.

I struggled to tame my memories, still replaying all those evenings, every nod of her head, every probing question.

Amanda said, "No. I really have no idea what you mean."

The ring of my cell started slicing through our back and forth — I ignored it.

The scent of cucumber from the kitchen candle crept in, normally the scent of cucumber had a calming effect on me, but it wasn't doing a damn thing to ice over the heat between us.

"Funny how things get clear in hindsight, huh?" I let my words hang, feeling the cool draft of my central air coming from the vents.

Her eyes widened slightly, and there was that silence again.

"Yo, I see you, Amanda. I said slyly.

I could detect a hint of nervousness in her fidgeting. Still, with her words, she kept her deception rolling along. "What are you rambling about?"

Any other week, I might've entertained her games, but not today. "Amanda cut the bullshit. I know what you've done. I just wanna know why?"

Amanda said, "I really have no idea what you're hinting at."

Before I could reply, she rephrased, "Or, as you might say, what you're getting at?"

It was the second time. Amanda was doing it deliberately. Talking down to me like I was some kid who couldn't comprehend her words. I felt the heat of my anger flare. It was more than just her betrayal now; it was also her condescending attitude.

But I held back, choosing to confront the bigger issue. I looked straight into her eyes, and I said, "Cut the damn act, Amanda. Just stop."

She touched the door handle. "Clearly, you're not in the right headspace."

As she started to open the door, anger boiled inside me. Bubbling over, I spat the question, "Why did you record me?"

She froze, her face white as snow.

I raised my voice. "Answer me, damn-it!"

The cell phone was insistent, a relentless jingle from the living room, where the low murmur of the basketball game played like it was miles away.

She tried to throw me off. "First, answer your damn phone."

"To hell with the phone, answer me," I shot back, the anger in my voice raising the stakes.

"Santé, I'm not going anywhere," she softened, closed my door, and took her hand off the knob. "I just don't want to keep yelling over that incessant ringing."

So I walked over, past the comfort of my couch, to grab the phone — Kay's name lit up the screen again. Fuck! I thought: that woman's got timing. She's already called like fifty times, and I've made fifty dodges. I know she lost her job, but I lost my promotion; we've all got problems. I didn't need another bitch trying to play the victim and blaming me. Whatever her deal was, I didn't want any part of it. With a sigh, I hit 'block.' "There, silent."

Returning to Amanda, I held onto my cool, but barely. "Why the fuck were you recording my conversations? No more bullshit, I want the truth."

She looked at me, all remorseful and shit, stuttering, "I... how did you... let me explain." She stammered, her back against the door.

"So?" I raised an eyebrow. "Spit it out."

Amanda hesitated, then finally confessed, "I'm working..."

Jumping to conclusions, I interrupted her. "Working for my ex-wife, right?"

Her shock appeared genuine as she responded, "What? No!"

"Then who are you working for?" I demanded.

Her eyes flashed wildly. "Nobody. I... I was gathering content."

My body swayed from side to side. "Since you like to dumb things down for me, stop talking in circles and just tell me the truth... if you know how."

"The content was for me," she said. "I'm writing a book."

My eyebrows almost touched each other. "A book... about me?" I asked.

Amanda rationalized, "You've always been a storyteller, Santé. I just never told you I believed those stories deserved a wider audience than hushed voices in my lounge or macho talk in locker rooms."

"And you didn't think you should ask me first?" I demanded.

Amanda hesitated, looking genuinely regretful. "I should have. I know that now. But it's about the things you told me."

"And that makes it okay?" I shot back, my voice dripping with betrayal-fueled contempt. "I said those things to you in trust."

She lowered her gaze. "I thought I could keep our growing friendship relationship separate from my work."

I was livid, and yelled, "You should've thought of that before you decided to play reporter with my life!"

Amanda's voice was unsteady. "I was blinded by the stories, your stories. But now I see how wrong I was."

"So, that's all I was to you? Just chapters for your book?" I asked, trying to grapple with the betrayal and maximizing her guilt.

"No, Santé," Amanda replied earnestly, "I care about you. I genuinely do. But I let my ambition blur the lines. I'm sorry."

I wiped beads of sweat off of my forehead. "Sorry? Is that supposed to make everything right?"

Amanda lowered her head in silence.

I stared at her for a moment. "You need to drop that book."

She looked at me, her eyes filled with tears. "Okay. I'll stop writing. I promise. It's not worth the anger and bitterness. Especially since we were getting to know each other."

I was feeling a mix of relief and residual anger. I decided to test the deceitful Amanda in a big way and shift the power in the process.

I walked to the base of my staircase, pulled my black tank top off over my head, and tossed it to the floor, quickly removing my red ball shorts and throwing them to the floor, too.

Amanda's eyes were practically on her cheeks as I stood at the base of my staircase naked. "If you're serious about getting to know me, you'll meet me in my bedroom... again. You know where I lay, if not lock my door when you leave."

I walked upstairs, my dick swinging with confidence. I suspected Amanda would follow, and I would be in the driver's seat. If she did, I would be in control, and the power shift would create a story more sexually explosive than she could imagine.

CHAPTER FORTY-ONE

STOP THE RUNAWAY TRAIN

My bare feet with polished pink toes met my red lounge's plush, black carpet. Each step I took was soft, almost muted, like a whisper. The carpet bore the imprints of countless evenings spent in conversation with Santé.

I recalled the many times Santé had sat across from me, relaxed, unguarded, sharing secret after secret; weaving the rich web of sex stories and narcissism that were supposed to be in my book—Santés Secrets.

With every memory, a fresh wave of guilt and confusion washed over me. My eyes scanned the room, first landing on the clock, 4 A.M., then the couch. How did he find out? How did it all go so wrong?

My gaze settled on a framed photo from high school—Isaac and me. The photograph brought memories of his infectious laugh, our younger selves seemingly untouched by the complexities of life.

Holding the photograph, I looked around the lounge aimlessly, my heart open; I could feel how much we'd grown, changed, and faced countless challenges together since that picture was taken, but tonight's hurdle would be unparalleled.

Taking a deep breath, I placed the photograph down and I picked up my cell phone. I dialed Isaac's number and waited; the drawn-out seconds amplified my anxiety.

When Isaac's voice finally came through, his drowsiness was palpable. "Amanda? Why are you calling at this hour?"

"Isaac," I hesitated, my voice low and measured. "We need to talk about the book."

A pause. "Did something happen?" His tone shifted, a note of concern creeping in.

Swallowing hard, I tried to find words, but they escaped me. Instead, memories of my time with Santé flashed before me: his stories, then his laughter, and our shared secret.

As I lowered my aching body onto the black couch, Isaac repeated his question. This time, his voice was louder and more demanding.

"Manda, I asked you, did something happen?"

Swallowing hard once more, I closed my eyes. "It's... complicated." I murmured.

Sensing my hesitation, Isaac's tone shifted from sleepy to sharply concerned. "Did you meet with Santé tonight after all?"

I remained silent. I didn't have the energy to lie to Isaac. My last attempt at deception about the meeting didn't work. Without saying a word, I heaved deeply. Isaac, knowing me as he did, began piecing it together. "Amanda, did you two...?"

With a shaky exhale, I admitted, "Yes, Isaac, he fucked me. Deeper and more intensely than I ever thought possible."

Isaac sighed heavily, a mix of frustration and sympathy. "I saw this coming, Amanda. I told you so. But I never thought you'd let it get this far."

I admitted, "Neither did I. I thought it was an innocent crush. I had no idea he'd have me face down, ass up, fucking me within an inch of my life."

Isaac's voice softened. "Wow. Under normal circumstances, I would toast to your escapades, honey, but this is not good."

Finally, I dropped the bomb. "The book is off. It can't happen."

"What?" Isaac's voice rose in both disbelief and anger. "The hell you say! I specifically asked you if you had any doubts. You told me no. I sent you the contract—you signed it."

Isaac then asked me, "You got the money... didn't you?"

Sittin' on the floor, I tapped my foot on the soft carpet. "I... I only spent eight of the ten thousand."

Isaac's voice shook, his frustration palpable. "You spent $8,000 in less than a month?"

"This operation has been expensive," I defended. "I could go into details, but the point is, I don't have the money to give back to the publisher."

Isaac asked, "So how the hell are you telling me you plan to stop the book after you've spent the money?"

I took a deep breath, my despair evident. "I don't know, Isaac. I was thinking that since you made the connections with the publisher, you could tell them I'll get a loan on my house and give the money back. Whatever needs to be done."

Isaac's voice was sharp and filled with disbelief. "Amanda—girl, with all the money involved and both of our careers on the line, are you willing to end everything just because Santé gave you the dick you once? Either your guilt is out of control or his dick was amazing. Either way, you're overreacting.

Pulling the phone slightly away from my ear, I tried to gather my thoughts. "First of all, it wasn't just one time, and secondly, I told you it's complicated."

Isaac yelled, "Well, dammit Amanda, make it less complicated than."

My heart raced. "He knows... He knows everything."

Suddenly there was silence. I could almost hear Isaac's mind whirring. Finally, Isaac's voice returned, a blend of disbelief and horror. "You told him?"

"Of course I didn't tell him, Isaac."

"How did he find out?"

I lay flat on the floor, sinking into the carpet—black as my despair. "I have no idea," I said.

"How did he tell you he knew?" Isaac's voice trembled with anxiety.

"Boldly," I said.

I could visualize Isaac rubbing his temples. "Damn."

"He made me promise to stop the publication of the book."

"Or else?" Isaac asked nervously.

"He didn't say exactly, but he implied he would do something," I said.

"Something physical?" Isaac asked cautiously.

I shuddered at the thought. "He didn't say, and I didn't ask directly. But if I had thought he was going to hurt me, I wouldn't have stayed. All I know is this is a mess."

I could hear Isaac taking a deep breath, trying to calm himself. "So, what exactly did you promise him?"

I tearfully said, "I promised him there would be no book at all."

Isaac's voice became soft and wistful, "Remember our high school dreams, Amanda? This book was supposed to be our uniting dream. And now?"

Tears fell onto my cheeks as the reality of my actions and their potential consequences began to sink in. "I know, Isaac. I never meant for things to spiral this way. But somewhere I got lost."

"We're in deep, Amanda. Excerpts are already with bloggers. The anticipation is building. How do we turn back now?"

Feeling the enormity of our shared dreams and responsibilities, I pleaded, "Isaac, we need to try. For the sake of what's right."

Our conversation lingered on, with Isaac emphasizing the original mission of our book: the exploration of narcissism and its dark ties to infidelity. We revisited shared memories, past challenges, and the essence of our collaboration.

Finally, as the early light of dawn began to emerge through my curtains, Isaac conceded, "Alright, Amanda. I'll do my best to stop the runaway train, but for now, rest."

Exhausted, I ended the call. The lounge, drenched in memories and the golden glow of dawn, seemed to embrace me. Thanks to the emotional vortex in front of me and the effects of Santé's sex marathon, I was spent mentally and physically.

I lacked the energy to make it up to my bedroom. So, I rose from the carpet and threw myself onto the plush red leather cushions of my couch. I felt submerged in a whirlpool of contradictions, trepidation, and regrets. I had no idea what would happen next, or precisely how I could influence it.

CHAPTER FORTY-TWO

THE RED GLOW OF JULY FIFTH

It had been a month since I had last laid eyes on Amanda, Kay, or that freaky bitch Holly. I wanted things to slow down a notch, and that's just what I got. I tried to keep to myself at work and especially to avoid Lee, the new supervisor, stomping around.

I had been thinking I'd hit up Holly for a good dick suck, but when she no-showed at both my basketball games, it read clear as day; not worth my time. I am Santé Sabatino after all, and one thing about me; I ain't the chasing type of dude.

So, I cashed in on some quality time with the kids instead. Surprisingly, Jackie decided to play ball. She agreed to a temporary setup, bringing the kids twice a week in addition to our arrangement for every other weekend visitation.

I had just spent Sunday, the 4th of July with the young bucks, but little did I know Monday, July 5th, would be the day of the biggest fireworks of all.

I was in the middle of welding a shipping container, Lee approached, hollering out my full name. It felt straight-up bizarre. No one had ever interrupted me while welding. Raising my welder's mask, I looked into Lee's smug face; I said. "Yo, what's up?"

Lee smirked and replied. "Joel wants to see you upstairs."

"Can't it wait till my break?" I asked.

Lee's glare intensified. "Now, Santé."

Man, ever since Lee took over, shit had changed. I thought about needing to look for a new gig, away from Lee's constant need to flex his power.

Heading upstairs, I saw Elaine in the reception area. She left her desk and reached for my hands. "What's up, darling?" I teased.

She shot me a nostalgic smile. "The big guy in the back sent for you."

She slowly parted her lips. "But first, I wanted to tell you something." Her voice was sincere; her glare piercing. "You have many talents, Santé. Don't let personal shortcomings overshadow your blessings."

Feeling off balance, I cocked my head. "You been hitting the sauce, Elaine?" I chuckled.

Her grip tightened. "You're special, Santé. Unique. Remember that."

I looked at her, feeling uneasy. "Why you laying it on so thick today?"

She sighed, "Just felt it on my heart. And also... I love you."

"Wait, what?" My eyes widened, but Elaine just sent me toward Joel's office, cutting short any response.

I passed Kay's empty desk. Damn, her firing felt like a death. The office felt off. Trina avoided my gaze. Yvette whispered, "Keep ya head up, sexy."

I nodded and said, "Sure thing, babe."

I knocked on Joel's door. Entering, I squinted, adjusting to the brightness. Joel's new office lights beaming from his ceiling made the office room shine unnaturally.

Joel motioned for me to sit. I looked at him behind his desk, an eerie red reflection in his glasses. I could tell it was coming off his laptop, but still, it made him look like he had laser eyes or something.

"Ah, Santé," Joel began, his voice was smooth, always so controlled. "Family and community, you know how much they mean to me. My church, my values. You get that, right?"

I forced a smirk. "Sure, Joel, I get it." But instead of ending the sermon there, Joel droned on for another five minutes about community values, company values, and some other shit.

Finally, I was done. Impatiently, I clenched my fists. "Why you preaching to me, Joel? What's this all about?"

Joel took a deep breath, fingers tapping on his desk. "Santé, I recently heard about... a book. I haven't read it, but I've learned about it from a trusted source."

"A book?" I asked, feeling a cold sweat forming at the back of my neck.

"Yes, a book that is apparently pretty scandalous. There are tales in it, things that shouldn't be in any book in my opinion. Disturbing tales, even tales from this company, from here, this very office."

Playing it cool, I chuckled, "A book? Man, there's a ton of those. Why should that bother you?"

"Joel hesitated; the lines on his forehead deepened; he turned his chair slightly away from me, then snapped back, "Santé, did you hear what I just said?" Joel's voice was strained, almost pleading. "The book is about you, and it includes my company, my employees, and my very office."

His glare remained fixed on me, intensity building. "From the small part I've read, this book goes into... certain behaviors, sexual behaviors. Things not fitting our values."

He took a deep breath, his chest visibly rising and falling. "It's tarnishing your reputation and, by extension, mine."

Joel paused, fingers tapping on the table. "There's no other way to say this, Santé, your name and reputation are becoming... radioactive."

His words felt like a punch to the gut. "So now you're buying into stories? Over actual people? I'm one of your best welders. A few years ago, when you had that big contract, I came in on my days off to help expand this damn company, and you're gonna play me like this?"

Joel ran a hand through his hair, looking genuinely conflicted. "It's not just the book, Santé. It's the talk that's sure to follow. This book is going to hit big. I'm a respected figure, a pillar in the church. If those stories taint that respect, everything I've built is at risk."

Joel took this heavy sigh and started messin' around with a damn pen. The room got real thick with a tense vibe, like something big was 'bout to drop.

He finally looked up, tryna lock eyes with me. I caught a faint red hue in his glasses, that same eerie glow that had been freakin' me out from the moment I sat down.

"Santé," he started, his voice all shaky, then the rest of his words were strong and hit hard. "Look, I'm truly sorry, but as of today, you're terminated. Effective immediately."

Man, it felt like I got sucker punched in the gut. Everything got kinda wobbly for a second. My ticker was racin', all this heat and confusion bubblin' up. I wanted to clap back, but the words got stuck. I didn't know how to even come back from that. So I just stiffened.

I looked at this red-eyed monster in front of me, and I was heated. I slowly stood up, exhaling heavily. "Man, you always talked about loyalty, and trust. Guess that's just talk, huh?"

His punk ass wasn't even man enough to look me in the eye; His voice was low, saying, "I wish things were different." If it wasn't for those cameras I knew were in there, I'd bitch slap his ass. Send those red glowing glasses right off his fucking face. But I had to chill. I lost my gig; I certainly didn't need to catch a case too.

Walking out, the calm hum of the office activity seemed like the whole scene was taunting me. As I moved to the open office area, all attention was on me. Yvette's teary eyes caught mine, turning up my pain.

I waved and said, "Peace out y'all." I didn't wait for their response, though I think I heard Trina say, "Best of luck, Santé." I know I heard Yvette's parting words, "We love you, Santé."

My inner voice was suddenly mad at everyone, including myself. "Santé, don't be a punk; you ain't going out in tears."

Approaching the reception area, I noticed Elaine standing by the swing doors, her arms extended. As I fell into her embrace, I felt a lump in my throat but fought the urge to break down.

Elaine's embrace felt good. Like the embrace that I didn't even remember I had longed for so many years from my own mother, who hadn't been in my life since childhood. Our hug lasted a while, and I needed it.

A few months ago, I was restarting my single life, a swinging bachelor with a good job, an excellent career, and a decent house. How had my life careened so far off-track?

As I moved away from Elaine, I reached for my keycard to clock out, my grip tightened around it as I contained my rage. I watched as Elaine mouthed the words, *I love you*. I blew her a kiss.

Pushing through the doors, I marched down the stairs to clear my locker, along with all signs that I had ever once worked at Manning & Mercer Containers.

Suddenly, like a bolt of lightning, I knew the answer to why my life had disintegrated into ashes. One name came into focus—Amanda. Just one goal became my purpose... Revenge!

*She fell into his eyes like deep water—
by the time she surfaced, she was already on her knees.*

CHAPTER FORTY-THREE

TWO CAN PLAY AT DESTRUCTION

Two can play at the game of life destruction, and since I was fired, I had nothing but time on my hands. I began to pace around my bedroom; my bare feet almost burned a path in my gray rug, and my desperation was as close to me as a second skin.

The passion for revenge pulsed through my veins with each thud of my heart. If Amanda thought she could fuck with my life, she had another think coming. My thoughts raced as fear tightened in my stomach. Yet, above all the chaos inside, anger roared the loudest.

Livid didn't even begin to cover it. Every footstep, every ragged breath was fueled by the seething fury towards Amanda Landry.

From what Joel spilled, I couldn't tell if Amanda's tell-all was already on the bookshelves, being peddled in the streets, or if it was just a hush-hush thing for the well-connected. But it didn't matter.

To ensure Amanda would pull that damn book wherever it was being sold, I needed her to see the fire in my eyes. She had to feel that I wasn't just blowing smoke; I meant business. Every ounce of my being screamed for action. If she wanted war, I was more than ready to meet her on the battlefield of betrayal.

I watched the footage of me fucking Amanda over and over for hours at a time. I wasn't sure which portion would make the best thirty-second clip to show her what would go public and how real shit was going to get for her if she didn't cooperate.

When I finally sat down to edit the video clip, I made sure to compile the highlights of Amanda sucking my dick; it was a mandatory feature. I made sure I picked the angle that showed her face the clearest. Next, I showed her sucking my balls.

Footage of me deep dicking her followed. I had closeups and all kinds of crazy angles. This looked so good somebody would think we were in a professional porn flick, some Platinum Pictures Inc., shit.

Once the video clip was ready, I uploaded it to a file-storage site on the internet cloud. Then, I sent the link to Amanda's phone. The fuse was set. All I had to do was wait for the explosion.

*She fell into his eyes like deep water—
by the time she surfaced, she was already on her knees.*

CHAPTER FORTY-FOUR

THE COUNTDOWN BEGINS

The pounding of my fist on Santé's entrance echoed like the sharp cracks of a starter pistol, demanding attention. Santé swung his front door open, and the blare of the basketball game spilled out like the crowd's roar in an arena.

He stepped back into his vast, open-floor-plan home, awash in neutral shades of gray and white.

Santé was clad in black basketball shorts and the yellow-and-black number 6 jersey he had made locally famous. His bare feet rested on the sleek wooden floor, a stark, commanding figure against the pristine white of the door he had just stepped away from.

He leaned casually against the support beam; his face showed a glimmer of triumph. "I knew that little video clip would bring you running," Santé said, with a challenging raise of his eyebrows and a smug twist to his mouth. His voice was almost lost under the sports commentary.

"You recorded us fucking?" I yelled over the commentators' excited banter, my voice sharp, "And you had the nerve to play the victim over my book recordings?" I could feel my face flush with anger.

Santé yelled, "Stop being so fucking dramatic. I only sent you the video clip. No one else has it for now. Your life hasn't been fucked up yet. But mine has."

I wanted to know what he meant by 'yet' instead I thought if he hadn't circulated the video, I should find out the basics of what was happening. "Santé, How the hell do you even have a video of us fucking much less sending it to me as some kind of threat?"

Santé's reply was as unresponsive as it was distracting.

He said, "You and your damn book got me fired, Amanda. With no job, the bank's going to snatch this house right from under me." His gesture took in the expanse of his beautifully modern five-bedroom home. "My success story," he said bitterly, shaking his head.

Santé then yelled a relatively incoherent rant about his boss, Joel learning of the video, being a religious nut, and firing him. Trying to keep up with his flurry of words was practically impossible but, the bottom line was he was unemployed, and my actions may have contributed to that.

I glanced around at the surroundings. His beautiful home indeed spoke of his success, but the empty rooms upstairs, devoid of children's laughter or a partner's warmth, also whispered of his failures. Now he could lose it all. A pang of pity, or maybe guilt, gnawed at me.

Confusion swirled within me; I had to ask, "Why would Joel even know about the book? Did you say something to him?"

Santé, with a snort, strode over to the sleek black couch and snatched up the remote, muting his 75-inch screen, quieting the basketball game mid-play.

The sudden silence felt like a vacuum, with no sound; I was drawn to the smells of pizza from his kitchen, mixing with the musty scent of used socks from a laundry bag near the door.

Returning to his post by the support beam, the lack of background noise made his words more pointed, more potent. He asked, "Do you honestly think I'd say anything to Joel about your little tell-all?"

Before I could respond, Santé continued. "No. Of course not, I don't know how he knows, but he knows and he fired me. Fuck! After all the catching up I did after the pandemic, for what? If I miss this next mortgage payment... I'm done."

His words pierced through my anger, injecting a fresh wave of guilt. I watched as he paced, his steps silent on the wooden floor. Although I was still furious about the video of us, I understood his anger and motivation for his freaking betrayal. What I couldn't understand was how his boss knew about the book.

In a daze, I gave voice to my confusion, "Santé, I don't understand, I told Isaac to stop the book. Let me clear this mess up." My voice was steady, but inside, anxiety swirled.

He studied me for a long moment, disbelief and skepticism etched on his face, then asked, "Who, the-fuck is Isaac?"

I hesitated; a cold dread settling in my stomach. I bit my lip, realizing my omission and the negative impression it gave. "Isaac is just a friend, a filmmaker who offered help. That's all." I insisted.

Santé pushed off the support beam, "A filmmaker?" he scoffed. "Were you going to turn my life into a fucking film? Some sorta reality show? And you're bitching about me betraying you? Seems to me my lil video just evens the score."

"It's not like that." I inched closer. "There's no film, no book, nothing." I insisted, then said, "Look, Santé, it's clear we've both made mistakes."

"Yeah, mistakes," he laughed without humor, "Sure, let's call it that."

Reaching Santé, and with pleading in my eyes, I said; "We don't have to destroy each other. I don't have to be at war with you,"

He crossed his arms, a statue of resentment. "Yeah? So, what now?" I watched as he began pacing again, his bare feet in constant motion.

"We can fix this," I said, though my voice was less confident.

He stopped and faced me, eyes cold as steel. "Fix it? You mean like how you 'fixed' your guilt of stabbing me in the back?"

I flinched, feeling the sting of his words. "It wasn't like that, Santé. But now, I'm scared... for both of us."

He scoffed, folding his arms. "Scared doesn't begin to cover it, Amanda. If your tell-all goes public, my life becomes an open book... and my chances of fixing things with Joel are zero."

"We don't have to let it go that far," I insisted, clasping my hands together. "There has to be something we can do."

His eyes narrowed, pondering my sincerity. "Maybe... But how can I trust you now, after all the lies?"

"Because I'm not your enemy. I like you, Santé, in fact, I—"

"Don't," he cut me off sharply, "Don't even say it. If the word love comes out of your mouth, I'll show you sucking my dick all over the internet."

I swallowed, choosing my words carefully. "Okay, I won't say love, but I don't want to hurt you, and I don't want to get hurt either. Do you think it's easy trusting you? Like you just said, you recorded me sucking your dick! A sex tape would ruin me professionally, not to mention the embarrassment. But I'm trying to trust you." I urged. "We have to be on the same team. There's too much at stake; we both stand to lose everything here."

He rubbed the back of his neck, displaying a flicker of vulnerability. He fixed his gaze on the basketball game, then finally turned back to me, his decision clear. "Here's the play: get me that publisher's number, I'll get a lawyer. They foot the bill, you torch the manuscript. And we make it snappy."

Once more, I swallowed hard, before asking "How snappy?"

His jaw clenched, he growled, "72 hours, Amanda. You've got 72 hours."

"Then a detente?" I ventured, a truce in my tone.

Santé shrugged, "I don't know what that means, Amanda."

I said, "It means I agree to your terms, 72 hours, that's Friday."

Santé's eyes glanced at the basketball game on his screen. He nodded, silently acknowledging our agreement. With the time pressure weighing on me, I had to gauge how firm he was with his ultimatum.

I gently pressed, "And if we can't stop the book within the 72 hours?" The question knotted like a stone in my throat.

"If you fail," Santé said, his voice low and resolute, "the world's going to see you sucking my dick and getting fucked... in high definition."

I gave a firm nod, resolute despite my tumultuous anxiety. "It won't come to that. I'll speak to Isaac and the publisher."

Santé's expression hardened, wary. "What if they refuse to listen?"

"They will. They must," I said, trying to infuse my words with confidence I wasn't sure I felt.

The energy shifted, a tenuous peace settling. "Is this the end for us, then?" I asked, the question laden with more than just our mutual sabotage.

His stare was hard, unreadable. "We disarm first. Then I'll figure out what 'us' even means anymore."

I sent him the publisher's contact information, my thumbs tapping frantically on my phone. "I'll talk to them. We'll align everything once you have a lawyer."

He nodded again, a truce etched in his jawline. "Good. And remember 72 hours," he said coldly.

Moving to leave, I hesitated at the threshold. "I'll get things set up

His smirk was a ghost of something familiar. He said, "After all this, Let's avoid words like setup."

I couldn't help but smile despite the storm we were navigating. "Fair enough. I'm just glad we're stepping back from the edge."

Grasping Santé's doorknob, our eyes met, holding a multitude of unspoken regrets. "I hope this works, Santé. For both our sakes."

He held my gaze firm. "Just get it done. Seventy-two hours."

As I stepped out of Santé's house, the sound of his closing the door behind me seemed to mark the end of one and the anxious beginning of another.

*She fell into his eyes like deep water—
by the time she surfaced, she was already on her knees.*

CHAPTER FORTY-FIVE

THE TEXTING GAME

The sports channel was blinking silently on the big screen in the background, but I wasn't really paying it any mind. I needed pussy, and I needed some fast. At a minimum, I needed the thing I valued most—getting my dick sucked.

I hated when my dick hadn't had action for more than ten hours because I had a tendency to fiend, especially if I was feeling stressed.

I got up from the couch and tried to navigate my living room floor. My once immaculate home was slowly turning into a maze for a game of hopscotch.

Clothes everywhere, man. Old shirts, jeans, underwear, you name it. Man, living the bachelor life was calm and peaceful most of the time, but the upkeep was starting to catch up with me.

The thought of having to hit up Holly first was a severe knock to my pride. Every alpha male knows you let the bitch slide into your messages first. But damn, things were getting desperate.

With no job, I could afford to waste no money on pussy. On top of that, what I really wanted was just to get my dick sucked. I knew I didn't have to spend money on Holly for that. Free dick-sucking would fit my budget perfectly.

It was official; I would text Holly. Straight to the point: Make the offer, take it or leave it, no games, no bullshit. But, I needed to think of a backup just in case ol' boy Jake was around and she couldn't shake 'em.

There was also the slight chance I could catch her in one of her moods. I damn sure didn't have time for that, so before I sent the text, I'd come up with at least five other options.

But first, a shower. I would've loved a quick swim at the club, but that, like a lot of other once-regular options in my life, wasn't on the menu anymore.

"Hey Babe,"

My fingers hovered over the phone, waiting for Holly's reply.

When she didn't reply in the first three minutes, I ran through my contacts; Janelle, Marissa, Jessica, and Abigail seemed like relatively good prospects.

(Text To: Janelle)
"What's up gorgeous?"

(Text To: Marissa,)
"What's up gorgeous?"

(Text To: Jessica,)
"What's up gorgeous?"

(Text To: Abigail,)
"What's up gorgeous?"

One minute at fifteen seconds, the first pull on the fishing line came in.

(From Jessica)

"Yo, you trying to get me killed. I told you never after 5 P.M., Thank god he's in the shower. I'm putting this on do not disturb."

There was no need to even reply to that; come on, contestants, how many of you are playing, who's sucking Santé's dick tonight?

Five minutes later:

(From Abigail)

Hey, who is this?

I thought whore. Doesn't even know how many dudes she's given her number to. The perfect kinda slut needed for the job. Then I texted:

(To Abigail)

"Santé!"

(From Abigail)

How long has it been?

(To Abigail)

You miss me?

(From Abigail)

Yes, for like six months. Why did you ghost me?

(To Abigail)

Lots going on. What you doing now?

(From Abigail)

Getting ready for work tomorrow, it's 11 o'clock. You never hit me up this late whatcha off tomorrow?

(To Abigail)

I go in late. Are you too sleepy to suck this dick?

(From Marissa)

"Damn, Santé?"

(To Marissa)

"Miss me?

(From Marissa)
Yeah, but I'm angry with you. I let you fuck me on my car hood, you nutted and pulled off, I ain't seen you since."

(From Abigail)
It's too late; I have to be up in a few hours. Maybe tomorrow.

(To Abigail)
Cool. Nite.

(To Marissa)
"Let me make it up to you, let me put this dick in your mouth."

(From Marissa)
You are so nasty.

(To Marissa)
Just like you like, right?

(From Marissa)
Kinda.

(To Marissa)
So, what's up.

(From Holly)
Hey, I thought you forgot about me.

(To Holly)
Never. Come out and suck my dick.

(From Holly)
I'm not at home, I'm over Jake's.

(To Holly)
So you can't get out like you did before?

(From Marissa)
Can we set up something for this weekend?

(From Holly)
Maybe.

(To Marissa)
I'll let you know.

(To Holly)
No maybe get a room; my dick is hard NOW

(From Marissa)
Cool Nite Sweetheart

(To Marissa)
Nite Babe, dream of me.

(From Marissa)
I will sleep tight.

(From Holly)
I'm broke. Can I finally come to your place? No wifey anymore, right?

(To Marissa)
I will now.

(To Holly)
Kids. Find the money. I wanna bust this nut in your mouth.

Five minutes later...

(From Holly)
Meet me at the motel in an hour, I'll text you the room number.

(To Holly)
Cool.

I thought: no more players, we've got a dick-sucking winner, a return champion—Holly. Gotta go!

CHAPTER FORTY-SIX

HOLLY, WOULD

"C'mon, eat up," I said, slapping my dick on her lips. From her knees, Holly's fingers lifted my dick, staring at my big, beautiful beast, bigger than her hand. A smile cut across her face. I knew Holly would do exactly what I told her to do. As Holly was getting high off of my validation, I considered givin' her the nickname 'Holly-would'. A good nickname for a good bitch.

I could tell from her quivering bottom lip, she had been craving my dick for weeks. That's why she paid for the cheap motel; she was seconds from getting her well-earned reward—my dick in her mouth.

She licked the tip of it. The light brush of her tongue across my sensitive foreskin was just right. I was semi-circumcised—had a mini-hoody, and Holly loved it. "Mmm," she murmured; her approval of the look and taste of my Puerto Rican Pinga made an emotional connection with me in a way I hadn't expected.

I said, "Good, right?" Then leaned back onto the motel bed, which had seen more than its fair share of secrets. I told her, "Let each lick remind you why you're here. You're not just sucking my dick, you're living your purpose, bitch, one lick at a time."

Her tongue seemed to borrow a secret from my past lover. A technique I taught Victoria. Holly's tongue carefully swept under the hood of my impeccably maintained foreskin, sending shivers through my dick and down my spine.

Holly's mouth watered, and she chuckled playfully, her sound so bright it seemed out of place in our grim surroundings. My pre-cum percolated at my tip, and she was quick to catch it with her finger. Playing with my savory sword, and tasting the flavor of my pre cum caused her to laugh, which provided a moment of fresh innocence in the otherwise musty and jaded room.

She held my dick with both hands, much like an ice cream cone. Her hands, strong yet delicate, clasped my manhood as if it were a lollipop: long licks and butterfly kisses, all with smiles and loving glances.

I laid back fully to enjoy an unrushed blow job from one of my most dedicated dick-suck roster members. My numbers had slipped over the years, particularly during my marriage. But including Holly, I still had five bitches that knew what they were doing.

Inside Holly's mouth was slick, warm, and active. Her suction started out as a soft nudge, then became a full wet vacuum; I was in heaven. For a while, all my stress, unemployment, and scandal disappeared, taken from me and stored somewhere in the back of Holly's throat.

Up and down, in and out of her mouth, as the image of the grimy ceiling faded under my eyelids. My entire body was warm. With Holly in the background giving me pleasure, my body's memory released images of women from my past. Some were as good as Holly, but most were not. The top three and the most problematic were better.

Victoria was by far the best dick sucker. I knew she had been released from prison, but I wasn't sure how a reunion might go. After all, she had shot me. Despite everything — the ups and downs, her sneakiness, my passion for revenge, I would always have a piece of her heart, and she would always belong to me. I would always be her first, the one she waited for. I took her virginity. I also knew she would remain the most fascinating woman I would ever know in my life.

Next, images of Jackie, my ex-wife, came to me. She wasn't the best dick sucker, but her pussy was tops. I did love her, and despite the fact I couldn't be just hers, she was mine; she was my only wife, and she gave me my kids. Our connection was eternal.

Last came Kay. There was a minute or two that I almost slipped into loving her. She was by far the freakiest bitch I've ever fucked with on a regular. She just wanted more than I could offer. I wouldn't say I liked how things ended between us, but sometimes things don't end as you'd like.

I was pulled back into the moment in the most unexpected way. I felt cool air on my dick; Holly's mouth was absent. Then Holly's voice broke into my world of one. "Excuse me, Santé?"

I opened my eyes to find Holly, her lower face wet with drool. With her eyes filled with submission, she asked. "Would it be okay if you looked at me when I suck your dick?"

"You want to do what?" I acted as if her question caught me off guard, but real talk, this wasn't new to me. The bitches were mesmerized by the swirl of colors in my eyes all the time. It gets 'em feeling some type of way.

Even though I wanted to just lay back on some chill vibe, she was topping me off, so she had earned a little eye contact. Initially, my gaze flowed back and forth between her pleading eyes and Holly's sexy lips, wrapped around my dick.

Then I stared directly into Holly's hungry eyes. I could immediately tell something was happening inside her. Her eyes widened, and the hand she used to cup my balls trembled.

I kept my eyes locked with hers, and Holly moaned into my dick like my jawn was a microphone at a karaoke club. I could tell she was cumming. Her body flinched, and she choked, trying to deep-throat me.

Giving Holly that small amount of attention energized her dick sucking so much, I knew it wouldn't be long before I would be cumming too. "Suck that dick faster, boo." Holly's head and hand worked overtime.

The special tingle started small, then washed over me quickly. "I wanna bust in your mouth," I whispered. "Umm-hmm," Holly mumbled. I pumped her mouth. "Move your hands, no hands." I insisted.

"Ahhh!" I was cumming, hard! "Ohhh." As my body jerked, I looked into Holly's eyes; they were wide, wild, but focused.

As I busted nuts in her mouth, I imagined she was experiencing tiny fireworks of my cum popping off on her tongue and hitting the roof of her mouth before sliding down her throat.

I don't know how much cum I spilled that day, because she didn't open her mouth until everything was gone. Holly licked her full, juicy lips. "I-I think that I ..." I didn't know where her stuttering sentence was going, but I cut her off. "I have to go." I then patted her on her head. "Text you next time. I said.

Holly's face frowned as I got dressed. She asked, "So, it's over?" I dressed faster. "Yeah, but text me to let me know you got in." I hit my truck's auto-start. Holly got up from her knees while wiping her mouth. "Damn, I might as well go back to Jake."

Holly's trifling behavior eased any discomfort I felt for using her for the limited roles she played in my life: a primary dick sucker and a secondary piece of pussy.

It was time to bounce, and I had my hand on the door. "Wait a second, let me get the door key card; I'm going to check out and get back to Jake." She chuckled and added, "I should; he paid for this room."

It was my turn to frown. "What?" I asked, genuinely confused. Holly picked up the room's keycard from the black end table. As she approached, she had a wide grin and explained, "I used his credit card." Damn, I thought, *bitches were foul as fuck.*

I opened the door; that sweet night air hit differently after Holly's blowjob. I hadn't taken two steps from the motel room before a man's voice came outta nowhere. "So, this how y'all doing me?" He emerged like he'd just ghosted out of the wall or something.

Fuck! It was Jake, number 12 from the Turnersville Titans, my former court brother, who had become just a sideline shadow. Man, I could've gone without this face-off.

Shit, my gun was chillin' in the glove box, just a hot minute away in my ride. Meanwhile, Holly's face looked like she'd literally seen a ghost. The warmth of her mocha skin was gone; her face looked as gray as the shades of a storm cloud. Her mouth was open, but no words hit the air. "Babe, chill, it ain't even like that." she finally pushed out.

Jake was all up in his feelings, looking like he wanted to throw down right there. "What's this, Six? You're tryna steal more than the ball now, Santé?"

He hadn't been a team member for almost two years, but he still knew my jersey number. He should, both he and his bitch jocked my moves on and off the court every game.

I leaned against the door, steady as a rock in a hard place. "Look, man, this is between you and your bitch." I didn't flinch; I just stared, calm and unfazed.

Her voice came in weak. "Jake, I can explain. I wanted to talk to Santé about getting you back on the team."

He wasn't having any of it. "At a motel? Bitch please! Who da fuck you playin'?"

The air was thick, charged like the last quarter of a game, and the score was tied. Holly asked, "If I was gonna cheat on you, would I use your credit card?"

Jake barked, "Bitch, you left me in bed to meet another Nicca." He snarled as he asked, "How the fuck I know what you'll do?"

Jake checked the scene, and the message was clear: this wasn't our court, and I wasn't about to let him score any points. "C'mon, Holly. Let's bounce," he finally spat out, all the fight draining from him, like he'd just missed a shot.

She lingered for a moment and shot me a look, her eyes a mix of worry and guilt. But soon, she trailed after Jake to his ride, that cherry-red Malibu.

My Suburban's engine was already humming. I took a cleansing breath before hitting the road, leaving behind Holly's dick-sucking lips and the drama with Jake.

As the streetlights cast shadows and I drove away, I thought it was probably game over for future blowjobs from Holly, but worse still, it also likely meant I'd miss the chance to stick my dick in Holly's ass.

*She fell into his eyes like deep water—
by the time she surfaced, she was already on her knees.*

CHAPTER FORTY-SEVEN

DETOX AND REDIRECTION

Dear Diary,

Santé Sabatino ruined my life. And the worst part? I let him. How did I let that happen? How did making him love me become the only thing I cared about?

Why was I so empty that I couldn't even be loyal to Jake? And Jake wasn't the answer either. I realized that when he punched me in the mouth after we left the motel. I fought back, but it still hurt. A lot. There was so much blood.

I spent two hours at the hospital getting stitches. The nurses asked if I wanted to press charges. I could have. Maybe I should have. But honestly? I just want peace.

Now I'm back at home with my mom, which feels like a step backward, but I know I need to figure things out. I don't care about guys right now. I'm going on a dick detox. I need to figure out who I even am before I go chasing after love again.

I turn 24 next week. No real job. No boyfriend. Just memories of a man I thought I loved—who fucked me and only looked back when he wanted to cum.

I don't know what comes next. I just hope it gets better.

Holly

*She fell into his eyes like deep water—
by the time she surfaced, she was already on her knees.*

CHAPTER FORTY-EIGHT

PRELUDE TO 3 PM

Chillin' up in my second-floor loft, kicked back behind the white metal gate like a king in his cage. From up here, I had a clean view of the living room below—big-ass screen TV, leather couch just sittin' there, soaking up the noonday sun. Quiet. Still.

Up here, though? Different vibe. The beige carpet, the white walls—it was my zone. My spot. Work happened here; plans got made. Just me and the soft tap of my fingers drumming on the black desk, waiting for my next move to hit me.

That tangerine candle's scent had crept up, slinking into the loft like a horny bitch on her knees. Outside, the sun was high, throwing long stripes of light and shadow across the floor—like some kind of cosmic barcode.

There I was, in my comfort gear: just some gray Hanes boxer briefs and a navy robe, my bare feet planted in the carpet like roots. I had my phone glued to my ear, a catalog of mindless melodies playing while I waited for Lance Whitmore, my lawyer, to take me off hold.

Then "Don't Tell 'Em" by Jeremih started playing, and shit, it was like a time machine. I was no longer in my loft. I was back in Victoria's small, dimly lit basement in Philly, the air thick with my youth and rebellion, and that song, always that song, threading through our secret freaky moments.

Her pretty lips wrapped around my dick were the highlight of many of my days back then. The way she sucked and played with my balls gave me a hard-on at just the memory. Victoria was the first bitch to ever make me cum just from getting head. Hundreds of bitches later, no one, and I mean no one, ever gave me head like Victoria Robbins; she was also the first bitch to suck my toes.

It was during those times that life seemed larger than... well, life itself. Back then, Victoria was my star, but she burned too bright, and when things went up in smoke, I blamed her for not playing by the rules. Her stubborn refusal to stay in her place fucked up the game big time, ending with a gunshot and prison time.

The track faded out, and my lawyer's secretary, Jill, brought me back to the present. "Attorney Whitmore is tied up on another line, but he wanted me to confirm a few things," she said, all professional and crisp. "Sticky Novels has acknowledged receipt of the cease and desist letter Attorney Whitmore sent on your behalf. The company has agreed to communicate its decision at 3 P.M."

"Understood," I responded, my voice a rumble of anticipation.

"Also, Attorney Whitmore noted your request to be on the call," Jill continued. "Normally, he wouldn't have clients on the line during these discussions, but seeing as this is not a negotiation, rather an update, he doesn't see an issue. He asks that you simply listen in, not participate. We can address any of your concerns afterward. Can you agree to that?"

I could, and I did. The call ended with a reminder of the scheduled 3 P.M,. conference call.

Once alone again, I grabbed my phone, tapping out a message to Amanda seeking confirmation that she had made direct contact with the publisher. Her prompt reply matched the information I had just received.

I texted her: "Let's hear their decision at the same time. Come here, my place 3.P.M."

It took three long minutes before Amanda's one-word reply hit my screen: "Agreed."

I exhaled, looking around my office area, feeling the vibe shift. The clock was counting down to that 3 P.M., call when everything could flip. Amanda and I were co-pilots in something already airborne—now it was just a matter of how hard the landing would be.

CHAPTER FORTY-NINE

3 PM

Amanda hit my doorstep right at 2:50 P.M., Ain't no shock she was on time, but the second she took just standing right at the edge caught me off guard. It's like she could feel the heavy air waiting on my side of the door.

Stepping in from the July sizzle into my cool living room, she dabbed at her forehead—a little dance of her fingers like she was brushing off the heat, or maybe shaking off more than that.

The vibe in my spot was dense, all mixed up with bad blood, heartache, some leftover sex, and mostly, a kind of worry thick enough to fist bump. I needed us to be clear, no crossed wires about what was to go down.

"You got your side all lined up for that three o'clock call?" I threw the question, keeping my tone even as we made our way to the kitchen. My black Nike flip-flops were in sync—a steady beat, clapping against my heels with each step we took.

"Yeah, they'll ring me right after they decide, just like you," she said, taking a seat on the barstool in front of the small counter that split my kitchen from the dining room. Amanda sounded sure, but that nervous tap of her foot was signaling a whole other story. I propped myself against the counter, a lineup of stainless steel appliances chilling by my side. Our phones were laid out in front of us, silent and waiting for three o'clock to hit.

I was standing in the heart of my kitchen, the very place where the day's drama was coming to a head. "You ready for all this to wrap up?" I asked her, pulling the orange juice out of the fridge and filling up a glass, each move a break from the tension cranking up around us.

"Kinda. Depends on what 'wrap up' really means," she replied, her eyebrows gently rising.

Just as I was 'bout to dig into the hidden meaning behind her words, Amanda's phone buzzed at 2:58 P.M., cutting through the stillness and straightening her back quickly. It was nothing but a text, and her shoulders dropped back down as soon as she saw it. "That's Isaac," she told me, thumb flicking over the screen.

I snuck a glimpse. The name 'Isaac' was on her phone. I couldn't help it; with the stakes so high, I needed to see that she was telling me the truth for myself.

She kept it real about who it was, and I respected that. I was all ears, wondering if this Isaac had the inside track, something that might clue us in on what the publisher was about to lay down.

Amanda read Isaac's beef about being sidelined out loud. Then something about bloggers agreeing to remove posts promoting the book. My mind split between hearing the words and the thought of bloggers getting ahold of bits of the book — that stirred me up, knowing there were bloggers out there flipping through pieces of my sex life for likes and clicks.

Most had pulled their previews, except for one blogger Isaac stamped as "stubborn." That's one for the lawyer to square away,

I thought, stashing it for later. The main event was what mattered right now. My fingers clamped down on the countertop, grounding me as the clock pulled us closer to decision time.

Meanwhile, Amanda's hands were all over her phone, like she was trying to decipher some code. "Hold up, Isaac shot me a link to the one blogger that wouldn't back down," she said, her voice tight. She tapped and swiped until her eyes blew wide open, and her face lost all of its color.

"Sup?" I pressed, feeling that familiar twist in my gut that said shit was 'bout to go sideways.

She was tripping over her words, looking like she was wrestling with what to spit out. Finally, she just handed me her phone. "You gotta see this for yourself," she said.

And there it was, the screen blazing with a red glare that hit me like a stop sign. Dead center was the headline with my name written all over it: "I know Santé's Secrets, and so should you." Underneath was a blog post spilling buckets of my freak shit.

The smut that wasn't nobody's business—like me dicking down bitches during office hours. I scanned the post and caught a bit of the dirt they were airing out, and damn it, I wanted to fuck something or somebody up.

"Damn bloggers." I grumbled. A wave of nausea hit me as my private sex life got thrown out there for internet trolls.

"Did you read the blog name?" Amanda's question drilled into my bubble of anger.

I said, "Nah, I missed it." Zooming in, there it was, a name that sucker-punched me… "Kay's Corner." It all clicked, like the last piece of a jigsaw or the final turn of a Rubik's Cube. The red glow I'd seen in Joel's glasses when he fired me now made sense.

A chill ran down my spine as Joel's casual praise of Kay's blog from the cookout flickered in the back of my mind, something about it being his daily read. And then his face when he fired me, claiming some trusted source had tipped him off.

"That's how Joel found out, damn! Kay's little 'side gig' was his so-called trusted source." The words tumbled out before I could shield them from Amanda's ears, the betrayal sharp and fresh as a new cut. Right on cue, the clock hand hit three.

My cell phone broke the quiet first, its ring cutting through the thick air. "Santé," Lance's voice came through just as Amanda's phone lit up. I half-listened to him, half-watched her, catching every subtle shift on her face, looking for the slightest hint to what was unfolding on her end.

Her expression, open and raw, mirrored the heavy verdict Lance laid out in my ear. When the longest sixty seconds of my life finally rolled by, I gave my thanks.

"I got it, Lance," I said, my voice low, setting my phone down with care, the gentle click of the phone touching the counter sounding like the closing of a final chapter.

Our eyes caught each other's and held tight as Amanda finished her call. "I guess you know?" Her voice had this bittersweet edge to it.

"Yeah, I know," I admitted, my words coming out loaded, tinged with a mix of resignation, while Amanda's eyes seemed to reflect something like relief.

There was a beat of silence before I added, "Some part of me figured it would play out like this."

"Amanda gently asked, "You think there's a shot for us, or are you too wounded?" Amanda's double entendre wasn't lost on me—shots and wounds ran deep in my history.

That question threw me, but the realness of my reply threw her more. I held her gaze, with a hint of mischief in my stare.

I fell back on my life's creed, and with all the truth and humor I had left in me, I laid it down. "Well, I live by one rule, and it goes like this: "There's nothing ever so wrong with me that a good blow job can't fix."

*She fell into his eyes like deep water—
by the time she surfaced, she was already on her knees.*

EPILOGUE
PART ONE

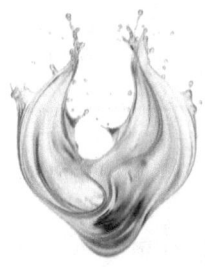

The liquid arms welcomed me with a serenity that permeated my soul. It had been a long and tumultuous week, with an ending that seemed inevitable yet still shocking.

The warmth of my bathwater contrasted sharply with the cold resolve that had settled in my heart back at Santé's house. As I lay in the murky mix of Marc Jacobs fragrance and melancholy, the memory of making that fateful decision played vividly in my mind.

It was right after the call from the publisher while I was sitting on Santé's barstool. The book had been canceled, and Santé's calm demeanor revealed nothing. But his eyes, those icy amber orbs, burned with a dangerous reality. The sea-foam green hues that once mesmerized me were gone, replaced by fiery red undertones—a volcano on the verge of eruption.

I knew then that our fragile truce, built on preventing Santé's secrets from being published, had expired. His retribution felt like a tremor beneath my feet, sending a shiver through me.

I told Santé I needed to inform Isaac about the publisher's call. When he suggested I call from his house, my heart skipped. Pretending to try twice, I told him I couldn't get through. "I'll Skype him from my place," I said, keeping my voice steady despite the turmoil.

Leaving his house, I felt his gaze, sharp and piercing. My heart raced as I crossed the lawn, grass crunching beneath hurried steps. Once inside, I grabbed my car keys with trembling hands. The garage door's loud creak intensified my fear. I drove to the police station, each turn of the wheel taking me further from Santé and deeper into an uncertain future.

The warm bathwater's embrace brought me back to the present. Yet, my mind drifted again, replaying the events at the police station—a final act in our tumultuous saga.

In the sterile interrogation room, I outlined the sex tape, the extortion, and the fear—speaking in broad strokes. The only detail I withheld was my recording of Santé, an omission that had the effect of a half-truth.

An hour later, the officers retrieved Santé. We sat across from each other, the tension thick enough to choke. His presence, once magnetic, now felt oppressive. Detective Marshall's voice sliced through the silence: "Ms. Amanda, can you confirm your relationship with Mr. Sabatino? "

"Yes, we were involved," I admitted softly. "But it's... complicated."

Santé's response was smooth and calculated. "I would agree; our relationship was complex. Amanda is a passionate woman. Our times together were always... intense."

I flinched inwardly, anger mixing with sorrow. How could he reduce everything to "intense"? I held back, knowing any outburst would only fuel his narrative.

Detective Marshall continued his probing. Then came the revelation. "We found cameras in Mr. Sabatino's bedroom. And the sex tape... with you on it."

Santé exploded. "That's it. I'm not saying another fucking word. I want my lawyer."

"Are you sure?" Marshall asked, unimpressed. When Santé insisted, Marshall shrugged. "Okay. We'll hold you a few more hours before charging you. Plenty of time to draft enough paperwork to bury your lawyer."

Marshall hoisted Santé up, and escorted him out. Santé's glare cut through me like a blade. Alone in the room, the chill of the station contrasted starkly with the warmth of my bath.

Detective Marshall returned, his presence breaking the oppressive silence. His questions were relentless, each designed to peel back layers of my entanglement with Santé. Beneath my composed answers, a storm of regret and pain churned.

Marshall leaned forward. "Mr. Sabatino alleges you recorded him for your manuscript. Both of you may share some guilt."

My heart sank. The recordings were meant for research, a project now abandoned. The irony of our mirrored transgressions stung deeply.

Marshall continued, "His infractions are more severe, but your actions aren't blameless. I might have a solution." He left briefly, leaving me to wrestle with the consequences of my choices. Was I to be charged for recordings tied to a canceled book? How had I fallen so far?

When Marshall returned, his words felt like salvation. "Mr. Sabatino is willing to forgo pressing charges if you do the same." Relief flooded me, tears springing to my eyes.

"I agree," I whispered, the words a vow to change.

As the bathwater cooled, the flashback faded. Rising from the tub, I felt a renewed purpose. The water had not just cleansed my body but baptized my soul. I had been given a second chance, and I was determined not to squander it.

*She fell into his eyes like deep water—
by the time she surfaced, she was already on her knees.*

EPILOGUE
PART TWO

Dear Diary,

I have a roommate now, and it's not a man.

I have a job, and it gives me more than just a paycheck.

I'm back in school in a big way, working toward a big career

Most surprising to me:

The desire for Santé is fading.

Plus, I've finally found love in the one person from whom I needed it most... me!

Holly

EPILOGUE
PART THREE

Anxiety and fear strung together sharply around my heart as the doorbell shattered the quiet of my house. A cautious relief seeped through me when the peephole revealed Isaac on the other side, not Santé. Despite our prolonged silence, I had informed Isaac that I was leaving Pond Drive a few days earlier.

The necessity of my move was undeniable, but it was the need within myself that guided my decision. I was ready for a change of scenery, a shift in existence. The flurry of confrontation and introspection that had filled the past weeks seemed to drift away as Isaac's warm embrace enveloped me. It was comforting in its familiarity.

I noticed the small paper bag clutched in Isaac's hand, its contents hidden by the curved handles. A spark of curiosity flared within me, but it seemed trivial against the backdrop of our renewed connection. I stepped aside, welcoming him with a wave. His presence felt new yet nostalgic; we drifted toward the lounge.

When Isaac sat on my leather couch, I noticed him observing his surroundings. Only then did I realize he had never seen the inside of my house beyond the camera frame of our Skype conversations. It was ironic, considering his involvement in the planning to acquire the property, and even more so now, as I was packing to leave Pond Drive for good.

A reflective tone colored Isaac's words as he asked, "So, this is where it all took place, huh?" I nodded. "True. He used to sit exactly where you are now." Heavy with unspoken thoughts, a pause hung in the air before he broke the silence, "Have you seen him?"

His name dangled unspoken between us, an echo in our shared stillness, yet unmistakable was our shared understanding—Isaac was referring to Santé Sabatino, the man who had fundamentally changed the trajectory of my life.

I confided in Isaac that I had caught a fleeting glimpse of him just days before; as I emerged from my car and he disappeared into his house, the silence was an eerie reminder of the finality of our brief yet cataclysmic relationship.

His question came softly. "So that's the only time you've seen him in an entire month?" My affirmation was quiet. "Yes, then, and the cold exchange at the police station."

Isaac's voice dropped a bit, and admitted, "You know, when you finally called me and told me about the book being canceled, I didn't catch a hint of sadness from you. That actually made me kind of angry. It hit me hard; I couldn't figure out why we had gone through all this trouble. I also wondered how it all turned so sour."

I gave him a wry smile. "This whole mess comes down to a few bad decisions, really." Isaac reached out, his tone soothing. "Hey, your heart was in the right place; you wanted to shed light on narcissism and infidelity and make it engaging. There's nothing wrong with that ambition."

"You had good intentions," he reiterated, but then his voice took on that familiar, clichéd tone, "though, you know what they say about the road to hell…"

That got under my skin. "You know, it really bugs me when people misquote that," I shot back.

"What's to misunderstand?" he questioned, a hint of challenge in his eyes.

I adjusted my posture. "See, good intentions aren't the issue—it's when one's intentions don't match one's actions."

Isaac's eyes asked the silent question before his words did: "Wait, what?"

I leaned in, making sure he understood: "Inconsistent intentions or intentions we don't really look at closely. That's where the real danger starts, and believe me, we had a showcase of that right here."

Isaac's expression reminded me of how I felt the first time I saw a calculus problem. I knew an explanation was needed.

I took a breath before diving in. "The first misstep? I was all over the place with what I wanted, with what I truly intended. I tricked myself into thinking that the end could justify the means—that I could mix a good cause or 'good intention' with some not-so-good actions."

Isaac agreed. "Yeah, I see what you mean, talk about a perfect storm for trouble."

I nodded again. "Exactly. Trying to mix good intentions with bad actions is like oil and water—they don't blend. I thought I could play both sides, but that was a losing game. You gotta pick a lane and stick to it, and I... I swerved."

I sighed, realizing the truth had more layers than I'd admitted to even myself. "It's the unexamined intentions that sneak up on you in life. For instance, I dove headfirst into this project without clarifying why I was so passionate about it. I mean, who buys a house and dedicates years to a story about someone they didn't even know existed before a chance encounter with a client?"

I saw the recognition dawn on Isaac's face. "Victoria, right? The woman you mentioned from your early counseling days?"

"Yes, that's right. Victoria's boyfriend was Santé Sabatino, and she was tangled up with Santé, something nasty. It got ugly; she shot him when he pushed her too far in some seedy motel. After she was released—thanks to a governor's pardon—I became her counselor. I used her story to track Santé without her knowledge."

Isaac's eyes widened slightly. "Wait, you told me about Santé and Victoria, but you never told me you created this plan, our plan, without her permission. You had her permission, right? You told me you had her permission."

I swallowed hard. "I told you what I intended to do. But once again, my intentions and my actions were inconsistent."

Isaac's face fell as the realization of my indiscretion settled in. "You mean you never got Victoria's permission to use any of the information from her therapy session to highlight the effects of narcissism in relationships?"

"No, she knows nothing about it because I never told her anything. At some point, I'm going to have to atone for that. But at the time, I was obsessed with Santé and the stories of his actions. I was also profoundly moved by the impact of Santé's behavior on Victoria.

"It was a mess, Isaac. She was lost, trying to piece herself back together, and during those sessions, she'd talk about Santé. I felt like I knew him, like his shadow had somehow cast itself over me too. There was this pull, this need to understand more about him. It was compelling and disturbing all at once."

I took a breath and continued, "I told myself I had a duty to ensure women knew how to avoid men like Santé. Although she was physically free of him by the time of her sessions with me, she wasn't completely free of him psychologically. None of us are truly free until we all know about these kinds of people and how to protect ourselves, which was my intention with the book."

Isaac's confusion was evident; "How is that unexamined? I only knew some of that information, but you knew all of it, and you knew it before finding Santé, so what was unexamined?"

Grinning widely, I tapped the side of my head. "You'd think so, huh? But here's the kicker—I chalked up my draw to Santé as some kind of cosmic curiosity. What I really missed was how it mirrored my past, my time with Pedro."

"Pedro?" he echoed, his voice rising slightly.

"Pedro was a whirlwind of young love. We were a thing just before you and I met during my senior year in high school. My infatuation with Pedro was the kind that blinds you."

My lighter tone contradicted the depth of what I was confessing. "Pedro was just as much a narcissist, just as much of a cheater as Santé."

I lowered my head as the memories and my realization merged. "Back then, I excused it all as passionate youth, the folly of being young and in love. It's easy to overlook dysfunctional behavior patterns when wearing rose-colored glasses."

I chuckled. "At first, I brushed it off, but I couldn't ignore the signs—I was heading down a destructive path. Just like Victoria, I was drawn into trying to fix someone unfixable. I got out before I lost myself completely. But when Pedro was ultimately gunned down, the guilt was overwhelming."

Isaac's concern was palpable. "Why guilt? You weren't involved in his death, were you?"

"No," I answered quickly, a little too sharply perhaps, and then softened. "I had nothing to do with it, not directly. I just... I had hoped cutting him off would make him rethink his choices. When it didn't, when his life spiraled to its inevitable end, part of me felt responsible for not stopping him."

"His reckless ways, that whole narcissistic lifestyle, it all caught up with him in the end. I used to think, if I could've just changed him, if my love could have made him different, maybe he wouldn't have died." I added, "I had nightmares about Pedro and his death for years."

A wry smile crossed my face as Isaac digested the weight of my admission. "Kind of arrogant to think my love could save someone like that, isn't it?"

He considered my question, and he looked thoughtful. "It's a lot, but I wouldn't call it arrogance."

"Thanks." Sighing, I added, "I think Santé's story triggered me. I convinced myself I had a shot at rewriting history, somehow saving him and easing my own guilt over not being able to save Pedro."

"So when did all the pieces come together for you?" Isaac's question was soft, probing the deeper currents.

"It hit me in the police station, but the realization started to unfurl on that Friday, July 9th, 3:01 P.M., to be exact, while sitting on Santé's barstool. The news had just broken—the publisher was out, cease-and-desist successful—and there I was, my professional dreams dissolving. Yet, a part of me clung to the idea of an 'us,' a couple."

"So I asked him about the possibility of a 'we.' I wasn't sure what I expected to hear, but I sure as hell was unprepared for his assessment of our delicate situation."

Isaac was all ears, anticipating the punchline. "He told me, 'There's nothing ever so wrong with me that a good blow job can't fix.' "

Isaac whispered, "You're kidding!"

I sighed and snorted lightly. "I wish I were. At that exact moment, in the absurdity of his response, I realized Santé would never change. He was a walking narcissistic erection, just out to please his penis."

"He was incapable of authentic change or growth—just as Pedro had been. Victoria had failed to reform Santé, just like Jackie failed. Just like I failed to reform Pedro. It was a pattern, one I finally saw with crystal clarity. I had to sever ties with Santé, not for him, but for me. Accepting that I couldn't mold Santé into someone else was the first step to reclaiming my life."

"So, from that point on, I knew what I had to do. It wouldn't be a walk in the park, but I had to set myself free by coming clean about what I had done and what he put me through."

A silence fell, Isaac's expression morphing into one of concern. "God, Amanda, I had no idea what you were going through." A softness came from his expressive eyes as he added, "Especially when I learned about... his tape of you. I owe you an apology."

"Why?" I countered quickly, then softened. "Don't apologize for Santé. You're not responsible for his actions."

Isaac reached out, his hand a warm anchor. "I know, and I agree. But I'm not apologizing for him. I'm taking responsibility for my part. I made your success my lifeline... and I've been terrified."

Isaac's confession hung in the air, raw and honest. "I don't know if I can be the independent film or television producer I've always dreamed of being. I think that's why I attached too many of my goals to your mission."

There's something else, Isaac confessed further, his big brown eyes suddenly glassy. "My mother's narcissism, her infidelity... I saw what it did to my father. I wanted to shine a light on that just as much as you did. It wasn't just about the money for me either."

A humorless chuckle escaped him. "Though the money is important, I truly wanted the story. I thought it was my best ticket to both my dreams of a future and a healed past."

"But now," he continued, his voice gaining strength, "your words are hitting home. Trying to do the right thing, in the wrong way—it's doomed from the start, isn't it?"

"Exactly," I affirmed. "If your intentions are clear and your actions aligned from the get-go, you pretty much set the course for how things will unfold."

"So what's next?" he asked, a note of hope threading through his words.

"Now, I'm selling the house," I said, the decision resonating within me. "I'll downsize to an apartment and start fresh. The sale might not leave me with much—this house hasn't been a home long enough to build equity. But it'll be enough to start anew."

His suggestion came gently, like a hand extended in the dark: "Move in with me, Amanda. We can help each other financially and figure out the future together."

I mused, "Good friends with good intentions." We shared a laugh that felt like the closing of a heavy door and the quiet click of a new door opening.

He delved into his bag, producing a small vanilla cake. "I know it's too late for a housewarming gift, but how about a celebration of new beginnings?"

I smiled; the future was suddenly not so daunting. "A new beginning to a life guided by good intentions and actions."

"That sounds like a plan," he agreed, then added. "Let's slice into this bad boy."

Nodding, Isaac and I walked shoulder to shoulder to my kitchen to cut into a cake of celebration, symbolically severing the ties to a past fraught with secrets and dysfunction. A new bond of friendship was formed, our hearts of one accord, sealed by the unspoken vow to never again mention—Santé's Secrets.

*She fell into his eyes like deep water—
by the time she surfaced, she was already on her knees.*

EPILOGUE
PART FOUR

I knew I had hit rock bottom when I was sitting outside Holly's apartment, and she had turned down my offer of dick. In some ways, that was more upsetting than a few days before when the police showed up at my door while I was waiting for Amanda to return.

The book publisher had just agreed to kill the publishing of that scandalous tell-all book, and I was trying to figure out how to make Amanda pay for what she had put me through. I had no idea she would take her betrayal and make it worse.

The banging on my front door shocked the fuck out of me. But seeing the police shocked me more. When the cops told me that I needed to come to the police station, I was humiliated and embarrassed. I hadn't been arrested or even detained since I was a young buck on the mean streets of Philly.

My suburban New Jersey neighbors hadn't seen the law come to my house since the incident with Victoria. But even then, I wasn't taken to the police station. Before I knew why they were there, I was sure it involved Amanda.

An hour later, I was slouched in a chair across from her in the cold, sterile interrogation room. The tension between us was so thick you could cut it with a knife. Amanda, once so damn captivating, now just looked pissed and defeated. She glared at me like I were the devil himself. At that moment... maybe I was.

Detective Marshall's voice broke the silence, sharp and insistent. "Mr. Sabatino, can you confirm your relationship with Ms. Amanda?" His question sounded so ordinary, but I knew it was loaded.

I glanced at Amanda. She wouldn't look at me, her face red from rage and hurt in her sad eyes. "Yeah, we were involved," she admitted; her voice was timid, and she appeared tired. I could tell our mess had worn her out. "But it was... complicated," she added. Like that even covered half of it.

I couldn't help but chuckle. "I'd agree; our relationship was complex, detective. Amanda here is a passionate woman; our times together were always... intense."

I dragged out that last word, watching Amanda flinch. She looked ready to explode, but she held back.

Detective Marshall kept digging, each question peeling back layers of our history, our twisted interactions. With each one, the room felt smaller, the truth tightening like a noose around us.

Then Marshall dropped the bomb. "We found cameras in Mr. Sabatino's bedroom," he said, looking straight at Amanda before adding, "And we found the tape... with you on it."

My heart skipped a beat, but I didn't let it show. Instead, I leaned forward, slamming my fist on the table. "That's it. I'm not saying another fucking word. I want my lawyer," I demanded, my voice hard and final.

Marshall's eyebrows shot up, seemingly more annoyed than surprised. "Are you sure?" he asked, almost like he was daring me.

"Fucking lawyer, now!" I barked, not giving an inch. "I want to talk to my lawyer." My demand was clear and cold.

Marshall shrugged with a smug smile on his face. "Okay. We can do that if you want to play this by the book. I'll take you to a cell. We can hold you several more hours before we have to charge you, and that will give us plenty of time to come up with enough criminal charges to bury your fancy lawyer in paperwork."

His words were meant to scare me, but I just leaned back, arms crossed, acting like I didn't have a care in the world. "Do what you gotta do, detective. I've got all the time in the world."

Marshall gestured to the officers, and they cuffed me, leading me out. I shot one last look at Amanda. Her eyes looked moist. I gave her a wink and a cocky grin. She could try to take me down, but I wasn't going down without a fight.

In the holding cell, I paced back and forth, my mind racing. I needed to stay ahead, keep my cool, and play this game better than anyone else. The detective thought he had me, but he didn't know who he was fuckin' with. I was Santé Sabatino, and no one was going to bring me down that easily.

Initially, the rush of victory was sweet. But I could almost taste the thirst for retaliation, sharp on my tongue, urging me to strike back at Amanda and whoever that Isaac dude was.

But as the adrenaline faded, reality set in. I remembered I didn't have the luxury of time or money to waste on revenge. Practical needs pressed on my mind—I needed a job and fast.

Beyond that, my dick had its own needs. The gnawing reality was I was super horny, and my roster of bitches had suddenly decreased, and with it, my options. The bottom line was I needed some pussy, good head, and to bang some tight ass. I wanted something straightforward and uncomplicated.

So, just before the cops reached the legal limit for my detention, Amanda and I had begrudgingly signed a mutual non-prosecution agreement.

The next night, I found myself standing in front of an unfamiliar apartment door in Sicklerville, New Jersey. In the small hours after midnight, my heart pounded not from fear but anticipation as I raised my hand and knocked on Holly's door.

Imagine my surprise when, after navigating through a sea of text messages full of detailed instructions on how to find her place, I realized the whole invitation was a sham. The come-on? Complete bullshit! It was just a plot to embarrass me, a petty game at my expense.

When Holly opened her apartment door, her stance was a clear signal. She didn't move aside to let me in; she blocked the doorway like a guard. I was thrown off. Foolishly, I rationalized that maybe ol' boy Jake had come home early. Perhaps we needed to reschedule, or at the very worst, he'd found out about us, and she was cutting ties.

But the truth was far simpler and more shocking. Holly didn't have a dude in there. There was no guy pressuring her, no extra complications. She had simply decided she didn't want me anymore. She didn't want my dick.

Then she hit me with a line that felt like a slap: "I'm not turning you down because I stopped loving you; I'm saying no because I'm beginning to love me." What the fuck does that even mean? I stood there, baffled and stung as she slowly closed her door on me.

As I sat in my Suburban, parked within view of her apartment, I couldn't shake the feeling that her words were just confusion. No bitch ever just walked away from me. She'd be back, I told myself as I stared at the closed door that had so abruptly shut me out.

I knew I had left my mark. The seeds of addiction were already planted, so she would be back. The thought clung to me like a stubborn shadow, giving me bitter comfort. Holly's eventual return seemed inevitable, and when she did come crawling back, she'd have to answer for her abandonment and disobedience. The idea of it, the reckoning—it was the only thing that soothed the sting of the rare rejection.

In the meantime, tucked away in a place I keep well protected, Holly's rejection truly hurt. Beneath the rugged exterior I show the world, Holly's words and actions had sliced through my defenses, carving a wound deep in my psyche. Especially after the drama with Amanda and losing Kay as a result of my own miscalculation.

I would never give Holly the satisfaction of knowing she hurt me in any way. That's why my last words before her door closed completely was, "That's cool."

I never told Victoria how losing her hurt me either, nor did I confess how my wife's cheating messed me up inside. Those painful emotions I buried, tucked away where no one could see them, where they couldn't use them against me.

Alone in my truck, I turned the key in the ignition, and the engine growled to life—a temporary escape from the suffocating silence that threatened to drown me. The sound was reassuring, a reminder of movement and life, even as my mind raced with heavier thoughts.

With my hand frozen on the gearshift, I reflected on lessons learned not long after my father passed away. Life has taught me, sometimes harshly, that there is a difference between being smart and being strong, just as there is a difference between being dumb and weak.

I'm smarter than I've ever been given credit for. I may not be the sharpest tool in the shed, but I'm relatively bright, and I've got street smarts, the kind you don't get from books, and that made me strong.

Over the years, I've been with women who were more educated than me, and honestly, I prefer it that way. Their knowledge, their way of seeing the world, challenges me and pushes me to think beyond the limitations of my own early childhood and teen years. I also learned a long time ago I had to be strong enough that I could fuck smart or dumb women and benefit from both.

Dumb bitches are for pure fun and filth. No boundaries, nasty beyond all morals. They can't offer much beyond the sex, but that goes a long way to stress reduction and ego boosts. You just have to remember to never get into any real relationship with a dumb woman beyond fuck, suck and run.

With the truck in gear, I wondered if I would ever write my own book with the stuff that really mattered—how do I stay strong, avoid weakness, keep my edge, and play the game? Love and lust is my actual playbook.

Love is Kryptonite. Sure, it feels good, feels right, but it weakens anyone who depends on love beyond self-love. The problem is that it softens people too much. Out of all the love I could give, I've only dished out three percent outside of me: one percent for my folks, one percent for my kids, and the last one for whoever's my wife at the time. The rest? It's all for me. Ninety-seven percent of all the love I'm capable of is turned inward, self-love. That's what keeps me sharp and keeps me on top.

On the other hand, there's lust. Man, lust is where I draw my power. It's simple—lust leads to sex, and dominating, powerful fucking is how I pull the bitches in. It makes both the smart and the dumb ones fall equally hard. The attachment to my dick makes them fall in love, and that's when they get weak.

As for me, I get the release of a nut, a rush that pumps up my ego, and a relaxation that eases my stress. The only catch is that lust is a quick hit—it doesn't stick around. It's strong, sure, but it burns out fast. I always need more.

As I pulled away from Holly's place and pulled out onto Williamstown Road, it struck me funny that Amanda had spent all that time writing a book on my life but couldn't pinpoint my real secret.

My Suburban's engine rumbled as I rolled down the small town road. The truck's noise pierced the night's quiet, and it all came clear.

My biggest secret isn't how I manage to fuck so many bitches, or the details of all the cum and cuties.

I pulled into my driveway and laughed once, bitter and low. My life had been a twisted joke I'd been telling for years. The punchline?

I'm just as addicted to my women as they are to me. I'm the one man they will be tied to for most of their lives, and I am chained to all of my bitches as a group. They will never be free of me individually, and I will never be free of them collectively.

That irrefutable truth is my most guarded secret of... Santé's Secrets.

ACKNOWLEDGMENTS

To the alpha males I have loved throughout my lifetime—thank you for allowing me to experience such a rich tapestry of fascinating traits, which enabled me to conjure Santé Sabatino with both bold authenticity and intellectual empathy.

To S.S.—thank you for our complex connection. You have changed my life in predominantly positive ways.

In loving memory of my father—his presence is profoundly missed, but his influence remains. Of the many gifts he gave me was his steadfast, nonjudgmental support of my creative endeavors. That gift remains among the most cherished. He was my greatest champion in my artistic expression, embracing even the work that pushed or redefined boundaries.

Thank you to the micro staff of Sticky Novels LLC and the dedicated collaborators who helped me bring this creative vision to life.

A special thank you to the team at CapriAGE—I'm so glad to work with you again. Your graphic design work has been an incredible blessing. You continue to translate my vision brilliantly, and I am deeply appreciative. Your work ethic and integrity are inspiring.

A heartfelt acknowledgment and thank you to Brady—your formatting skills and talent are superb, and your integrity and compassion make your contributions all the more fulfilling.

To my brother, Rome—thank you for your unwavering support and love. You remain a source of strength and stability in an ever-unstable world.

I extend my deepest appreciation, gratitude, acknowledgment, and love to Aunt Sis, Big Brother Gino, Juliet, Janita, Special K (Karen), and Dallas.

—Jade Green

ABOUT THE AUTHOR

JADE GREEN MADE HER PUBLISHING debut with Pyrrhic Victoria, a provocative and intricately woven exploration of psychological and erotic themes. With Santé's Secrets, she continues to push boundaries, crafting immersive narratives that blend psychological depth with compelling storytelling. Before turning to publishing, she spent two decades writing, producing, and directing independent films and television, bringing bold and imaginative stories to life.

Follow Jade:

SIGN UP FOR STICKY NOVELS NEWSLETTER!

Be the first to learn about Jade Green's latest novels, projects in developments, book discussions, Interviews and exclusive content.

StickyNovels.Com

www.ingramcontent.com/pod-product-compliance
Lightning Source LLC
LaVergne TN
LVHW031807080526
838199LV00100B/6345